BARBARA

BARBARA

A Novel

JONI MURPHY

ASTRA HOUSE ⋀ NEW YORK

Epigraph from "I Live in the Twentieth Century",
from *Trout Fishing In America, Pill Vs Springhill Mine Disaster,
In Watermelon Sugar* by Richard Brautigan.
Trout Fishing in America copyright © 1967 by Richard Brautigan.
Copyright renewed © 1996 by Ianthe Brautigan Swenson.
Used by permission of HarperCollins Publishers.

For information about permission to reproduce selections from this book, please
contact permissions@astrahouse.com.

This is a work of fiction. Names, characters, places, and incidents are products
of the author's imagination or are used fictitiously. Any resemblance to actual
events, locales, or persons, living or dead, is entirely coincidental.

Astra House
A Division of Astra Publishing House
astrahouse.com

Printed in the United States of America

Library of Congress Cataloging-in-Publication Data

Names: Murphy, Joni, 1980- author.
Title: Barbara : a novel / Joni Murphy.
Description: First edition. | New York : Astra House, 2025. |
Summary: "A radiant novel tracking the lifecycle of a silver screen starlet rising
against the backdrop of the mid-20th century"-- Provided by publisher.
Identifiers: LCCN 2024043321 | ISBN 9781662602870 (hardcover) |
ISBN 9781662602887 (ebook)
Subjects: LCGFT: Novels.
Classification: LCC PS3613.U7426 B37 2025 | DDC 813/.6--dc23/eng/20240920
LC record available at https://lccn.loc.gov/2024043321

First edition
10 9 8 7 6 5 4 3 2 1

Design by Alissa Theodor
The text is set in WarnockPro.
The titles are set in TrioGrotesk-Bold.

I live in the Twentieth Century
and you lie here beside me.   You
were unhappy when you fell asleep.
There was nothing I could do about
it.   I felt helpless.   Your face
is so beautiful that I cannot stop
to describe it, and there's nothing
I can do to make you happy while
*   you sleep.*

—RICHARD BRAUTIGAN

BARBARA

To feel the subtle grain of a moment, that is the goal, to be present.

I roll my thinking back. I return the years of sensation and numbness, the deaths and repetitions onto their reel. I start again.

Sometimes what happens to you does not make you better, it's just what happens.

I am forty years old, acting in a western in a town high up in the Rockies. Out in the world it's 1975, but in our film we're living through the ragged end of the gold rush. My scientist father died in summer. It's fall now and I'm toiling away as a movie whore. Outside yellow-brown aspen leaves tremble in the cool wind but I have spent the day inside on a stage, performing for the benefit of the camera. Inside the theater a spotlight makes a false full moon on the deep red curtain. I can't see it but I know the light is there. Velvet folds separate me from the others. Anything could be on the other side. I feel the geological layers of this time. The dark of this theater is so complete we could be miles underground. It's been years since I've felt the bright light of the sun.

A record spins on the phonograph. It is very important to Tony that the layers of sound overlap organically. There are many hidden mics to catch the chairs as they squeak and glasses as they clink. The other cast members playing miners and whores, they whisper. They move their leather heels on the wooden floor.

We've been listening to this aria again and again. The needle kept getting replaced back at the beginning. It's a part of the picture. At the beginning the soprano produces a rickety sound, but then she builds to something else, deeper and older, and yet more modern all at once. We hear the hiss of the recording mechanism, a woman's breath, then the fluttering of leaves rustling. It is so eerie and beautiful to hear her solo voice in a large echoey room.

We are communicating something in this scene, not about the music but about space itself. The space within theater walls is one of the dark wombs where souls nestle, watching the flickering of the past. Every movie is a record of a lost reality.

What the camera sees: The spotlight moon dead center of velvet night; delicate hand at the end of a slim arm appearing from between the curtains; spinning dust particles catching in the light's beam. Though the hand and arm emerge, the body does not follow. I am not made whole. I reach out, grasp and let go. I make a come-hither pull of my index finger. My hand floats like a leaf. It is the hand of a hidden nymph in a baroque painting. It gestures with a receptive turn of the wrist.

Feelings, nothing more than feelings. I hum to myself. It's been such a long history and there's still so much more to go.

Tony calls out once more, quiet please on set.

6

We're ready to go. Sound, he asks. Camera? Speed.

I reach once more into the dark.

After the day's shoot I go to my room and lie on the brass bed's sagging mattress. The walls around me are covered with flocked paper. The pattern is smooth green alternating with textured fuzzy vines that run vertical like cell bars. It's worn away where the headboard has rubbed.

The room is in the back of the hotel. I have one big window that looks out at the upward slope of the mountain, on which many evergreens grow. The window goes up and down on a chain, it free-falls like a guillotine if I don't prop it open with a stick.

Most times when I'm not needed on set I nestle here. There is nowhere else to go in this ghost town. In daylight hours I read and write letters, drink tea, and watch the trees move, warm beneath my down comforter but my hands and head cold from the air that creeps in. It's getting colder and colder as the days go shorter. When night falls the window goes dark, reflecting back to me the inside of the room. I see in it myself, or at certain moments, Jake and I together.

Jake Doherty is from Odessa, Texas. He has a way of rubbing his thighs with his palms, smoothing his long legs out in front of him when he first sits down. It kills me. He learned how to saddle a horse and handle a shotgun growing up, but all he's used his knowledge for is to act like a cowboy in movies. His father is disappointed, he tells me. But everyone else can't get enough.

Sometimes when he kisses me he wraps his hand around my neck. I wish whatever he had didn't work on me, but it does. He is my co-star and he has been coming to my room almost every night. I am playing a whore after all so what we do could be called a part of our method. I watch his shoulders reflecting broad and tan in the window and the sight of him, let alone the feeling of his skin, sends me into a trance.

Look me in the eyes, he orders as he pushes in. And so, I do.

It's not just sex though, but the time after. There is a special sweetness to being with him. Often we'll lie side by side talking, or being quiet as we listen to one of my records. We are fragile together. Jake is younger than me by years. He has his depressed wife in Laurel Canyon and I have Lev. But it doesn't matter. We are both beautiful and far from real life. We have the pleasure of disappearing into our fiction.

Jake lies on my bed blowing smoke at the ceiling. Mozart, he says, was irreverent. People think classical music is so serious but what they don't realize is Mozart loved dirty jokes. He was the perfect child of the world. When he was alive the people around him didn't know his work would come to define European culture. To them he was simply a bratty genius who couldn't hold down a job. But then, after he died, the whole of Europe somehow decided, this is how we sound, his art represents who we are. Not all the muck and mire, but the trills channeled by a playful boy.

Listening to music with another person can feel so intimate. Taking sips of brandy while a record spins in a dim room, while outside the winds blow the leaves off the trees, can make you feel like you really know a person, even if you've met only weeks before.

I tried to describe to Jake the loops my life had traced. There's no big climax, I said. My mother did die when I was thirteen years old. That's one thing I suppose.

She was thirty-six when she died. I was not living with her at the time. I was in junior high school, living with my aunt Marie at her home in Grand Junction, Colorado. My mother was at a clinic for mental health in sunny Pasadena.

In the mornings before school, I liked to read while drinking a cup of Postum with milk. I pretended it was coffee. It made me feel like an adult. I held my spoon like a cigarette as I skimmed headlines about pacts and invasions and polio. Marilyn Monroe was on the cover of *Life*. I remember reading all about her the morning I found out.

I was with my aunt because my mother was in the midst of a breakdown. Or as my father phrased it, she was taking some time to get her strength back.

At first my aunt told me it was an accident. Later though, I found out that my mother slit her own throat with a razor blade. That is no kind of accident. She hid it among her beauty products. I learned that somehow.

I picture even now the blade wrapped in its paper envelope tucked under the powder compact, beside the lipsticks in their glossy black tubes. She always kept her vanity case tidy. I used to admire the print of the fabric that covered the outside, a tangle of roses with thorny stems.

I remember my mother and aunt having afternoon drinks the day she dropped me off at Marie's house. My mother had her feet pulled up beneath her big blue skirt. Her leather pumps rested beneath the coffee table, one stood while the other was toppled over. My mother held her cheek with her head askew, as if it was too heavy a burden for her neck.

It's natural to want to remember a person as they were, especially if that person is your mother. She was framed by the couch back and behind that a picture window filled with trembling gold leaves. The leaves were yellow because it was fall. The leaves shook because there was a breeze. Through the screen door came the chill of that softly moving high-altitude air. It smelled sweet, in that decomposing way, and it kept the aspens shivering. My mother looked like a painting or a woman in a movie.

I didn't know it until years later when I read some of her letters, but my mother was pregnant then. Maybe that's why she looked so pretty.

I remember my aunt nodding, my mother waving her cigarette around as she talked about my father. She thought he deserved more recognition.

My father was an engineer who worked on the atomic bomb. He wrangled dangerous material for the government. He was one of those men of science the newspapers talked about. When I was young it was all a big secret, but by the time I came to Marie's the whole world knew. He belonged to something famous.

His mentors were serious and abstract thinkers who came from big universities like Princeton and Oxford. My father had started out at Kansas State College and so had a kind of inferiority complex, my mother thought. He was in the shadow of others even though he was so handy and had brought himself up in the world through his own brilliance. My father got mad when she said such things. He was proud to have any role in something so important as nuclear discovery.

He did what was needed with his entire capacity. Where the government hand pointed, he went. Or rather, he went and we followed. If ever my mother questioned why we had to move, my father referred to the defense of the nation. He did not merely work, he was assigned. He'd speak one of his incantations: I have no choice; I've got to do it. Even though the war was over, another was brewing and we had to be ready.

Though they argued, my mother still passed on to me my father's imperatives. Be quiet. Don't share too much. When you're a grown-up you'll understand why. Loose lips sink ships, repeated my mother, which I thought was a strange saying because the ocean was so far away from where my father had brought us to in highest New Mexico.

———

We moved around a lot during my childhood, but my mother never stopped striving for beauty and order. She wanted things to be nice, no matter where we were. It drove her crazy I think.

She scrubbed mold from the bathroom walls of our place at the Idaho Falls army base. She swept our desert porch with a fervor even though the whole landscape was dusty and it was going to blow back. The futility didn't matter to her. She cleaned and I helped her because I was told. After washing the floors she'd shake out the broom and bleach the mop. Pristine was how she wanted life. She used to say it was her German ancestors coming out, though later on she stopped using that turn of phrase. My father said people might get the wrong idea.

After each move my mother unwrapped the hurricane lamp and put her paper flowers in a nice arrangement. She sheltered her special objects and didn't let them get broken no matter what. She accented our government-issue sofas with mohair throws.

Unlike some of the other women brought there because of the lab, my mother loved New Mexico right away. Even with the dust she loved it. She'd spend our drives between Los Alamos and Santa Fe pointing out red rock formations, the blueness of the sky, and the whiteness of the smoke as it rose from a heap of burning brush. Down in the old capital we'd eat lunch in an old place with thick beams for a ceiling and then she'd buy things from the women with blankets spread around the edge of the plaza. She bought silver bracelets for her wrists and baskets woven out of pine needles to hold her jewelry when she took it off at night.

My mother was beautiful in the way the magazines wanted women to be. As a girl I was proud she was mine. She had blond hair, open blue eyes, and a precise and delicate profile. In all her portraits she had a head tilt. But even caught off guard in a snapshot, she had no bad angle.

My mother rarely hit but when she did it was hard. She could become enraged over things I could not predict. Her hitting felt impersonal, something that happened rather than something she did. It passed through her like an involuntary shudder. The anger then dissolved. She'd pull me to her breast then. My red cheek would go wet with a gush of her tears. She always cried more than me, even when I was young. She sobbed as if she were breaking apart. I'd end up comforting her. I'm sorry Mama, I didn't mean to. I'd inhale. I just can't bear things like other people can, she'd say.

I could never help but love other people smoking because it reminded me of her smell: Dove soap and light sweat, Lucky Strikes and L'Air du Temps.

At my mother's memorial there was nothing of my mother to see. She was absent except in the form of a photograph in a silver frame. Her. Young. Before me. Nothing haunted that room except a lonely feeling and the smell of cleanser. She would have liked that at least.

My father had my mother cremated in Pasadena and the ashes sent back by train. He had them. He said he was going to scatter them whenever he could decide on the right place. Maybe in the canyon where we went on those walks, my father said. I'm sure she would want to be laid to rest near you, my aunt said with a nod.

The memorial was proper because Aunt Marie made it so. The room was a rented meeting room, beautified with draped folding tables and flowers. I helped arrange the food. There were chicken sandwiches and pimento spread sandwiches cut into tiny triangles. Some macaroni casserole and a plate of pickled vegetables with a box of toothpicks beside. There was a cheese log encrusted with slivered almonds, crackers, date rolls, and sliced apples. Someone had made a bunt cake and a crumbly topped coffee cake. They sat beside an urn of coffee. Marie made an alcoholic punch for anyone who wanted to take the edge off. The smells all mixed into a generalized air that made me sick.

When my parents' friends came they drank down all the coffee, and ignored the food as it went stale and crusty. I could have told Aunt Marie they'd do that. My parents' friends mostly smoked. They were all too smart and elegant to eat.

We did not have crosses or music because my father did not believe in God. The only sounds were hushed voices and a box fan. Bouquets of white and pink and blue flowers stood up straight in glass vases. They didn't smell of anything. They had good posture like my father's friends. The flowers and the men talked only to their buddies, those who were like them, about serious matters that were not my mother. I pushed my nails into a green foam block that held spears of gladiolus. They were arranged in the foam inside a basket shaped like a shell. I wondered if I might be able to keep the basket after the flowers went bad, but I didn't want to ask for it.

My aunt told me to stop messing it up and show some respect for my mother's memory. She told me to go join my father, who was standing still in the corner, flanked by two of his friends. He spoke words to the wives who approached, never changing his expression, and then the wives would leave and he would go back to speaking with the men. My aunt told me to go stand with him but I couldn't. After a few more nudges she gave up.

The walls behind the bouquets and the people were curtained. The curtains were so thick you couldn't even guess where the windows were, or even if there were windows at all. We could be in Antarctica. We could be on a submarine, or in a bunker. We could be in a movie theater, I thought.

Outside I knew the sun shone and a breeze blew down from the mountains. The foothills out there were a soft orange color and still spotted with heaps of snow in the shady parts. The mountains were purple and white at the peaks. Snow, even in May. It was because of the altitude, my aunt said. I imagined no human ever went to those great sparkling heights.

I wanted to go outside, but also to be respectful. Be a good girl, I told myself. Like this the hours passed. Aunt Marie's face grew puffy so she hid it behind her blue handkerchief. She talked to everyone in a way that was uncomfortable for my father. His eyes shifted to her and away. She foisted plates heavy with snacks into the hands of scientists. They didn't want what she was offering. She talked in their direction about my father when he was young. With another couple she blubbered with memories of my mother. She grabbed for a man's shoulder when she stumbled off her heels. I hovered at her elbow, wanting to put a stop to all that made me so ashamed.

The only person who liked Aunt Marie was Renata. Renata was my mother's best friend. I remember I'd eavesdropped when Renata stopped by to visit with my mother. I'd work on my paper dolls on the living room floor while they drank coffee, smoked cigarettes, and ignored the cake my mother set out to be a good hostess. They'd talk and talk like I wasn't there. Renata's children were older than me and in boarding school. Renata liked to talk about her old life and my mother loved to listen. Renata had been raised in Paris. Her father was an industrialist and her mother an artistic Hungarian. She'd had tutors and attended a convent school. She knew how to play the piano. She'd attended dinner parties where Einstein was also a guest. She'd had rendezvous under streetlights, steamer voyages, and a first husband who'd won a Nobel Prize and then died straightaway.

Everyone liked Renata but she didn't like everyone. She chose my mother for her company. They'd become friends as soon as we arrived on the hill. She and my mother tried to start a garden together but neither of them knew what to do. They studied magazine articles about vegetables. This soil was hopeless, Renata said. She wanted herbs and flowers. Renata joked that her dear mama, who had luckily died before all this horror, would faint to see her daughter in dirty jeans, scraping around zucchini vines. Her daughter, a peasant.

Renata gave my mother a tube of rose-scented lanolin when her knuckles cracked from the dry air. She told me I'd meet her daughter one day, but I never did.

Renata called our town a mud pit and a military coop surrounded by wire fencing. Nothing here but us chickens, she laughed. But she also adored the great western vistas. She said some of the scientists and their wives had communist sensibilities. Even though no one was allowed to admit that, it did make the whole project a bit more bearable. Look at us, she laughed, all in it together.

At the memorial Renata embraced me and I let her. She rocked me back and forth and kissed the top of my head. My poor child, she whispered. Poor, poor baby. I wanted to keep breathing in her smell, her perfume and smoke and warmth and powder.

I wanted it to go on until my heart stopped hurting but Renata's husband Michael, who had not won a Nobel Prize but was still brilliant my father said, came up and whispered in her ear. They had to be getting along, as the drive back home was tiring. Renata let me go gently. I didn't cry.

I never saw Renata again. For years after the memorial, she sent me a birthday card with five dollars tucked inside. She wrote that I should buy myself something beautiful. The last one came when I turned twenty. After they stopped I thought maybe she considered me too old for this tradition, but Aunt Marie told me Renata had died in a car accident and that was the reason.

Maybe it's the mountains that have got me thinking about my mother. How I've become similar to her. I wonder, though, if I even know what she was like. I have to handle my memories carefully to keep them from disintegrating, they've aged while she hasn't. I worry each recollection shreds her a bit, but I can't help myself. I've wound up back where she left me in the Rockies.

I've been talking too much but Jake is receptive in the way a temporary lover can be. We have nothing to do besides rehearse and perform, make love and sleep, drink and tell stories.

Before my mother, I say, was my grandmother, who came over, pregnant and unwed, on a boat. And before her were generations of thwarted women who lived and died in Germany. That's what I know. When I think of my ancestors all I imagine is women getting trampled and trampling others. The grass they walked on every day grew over buried bodies. They picked their way between gravestones to get to the market and then they got sick and died and their daughters made their way through the same graveyard. That went on and on for dimly lit centuries until my grandmother came to America. Then, as soon as she arrived, America went to war in Europe.

My father said peace was imminent. He said the bomb would make war impossible. But then there was Korea, and then the missile crisis, the assassination that made people lose their minds and weep in the streets. We observed funerals while still dressing in matching sets, our hands in white gloves, and on our heads, little hats. Whole cities burned and so did the bodies of people still alive as they burned. By the time we were really in the next horrific war I no longer spoke to my father about the possibility of peace, or much else. There was, as they say, a crisis of confidence.

By logic I know I have descended from men and women who struggled to stay alive long enough to give life to children. That's the whole point people tell me. It's natural, yet I have chosen to spit in their eye and remain childless. I've gone further even than that to abort would-be children. I had two abortions for God's sake. My husband Lev says that I'm not cut out for motherhood and that I shouldn't fret so much, for sanity's sake. But he already has children from his first wife. He doesn't have to worry about disappointing the ancestors that came before.

My two stepchildren want nothing to do with me. They sweep by when I open the door, dropping their bags and coats when they come home for holidays. When I speak at dinner they scoff at my opinions. Lev's son Michael is, I think, attracted to me. I have felt his overheated looks when my blouse is unbuttoned too low. I can feel how that tension makes him disgusted at his father's decision to remarry, and so quickly after their mother. Not that I blame either Lev or Michael. I am in name stepmother, but no one takes that seriously, least of all me. I was roughly between Lev's age and his children's when we got married and I have dieted to stay thin enough to fit within this fold of time. I want to stay girlish forever. Just because it's impossible doesn't mean I won't try.

My mother, my aunt, even my grandmother, they all whispered about camps and lampshades made of skin and ships overfull of refugees. Human horrors stole all their attention. They talked about the world because through it they could mourn themselves. As a child, I listened. There were men in our family who died in war, choking in foreign mud, or because they got torn up by shrapnel. The women spoke of them. They warned me about measles, mumps, rubella, and iron lungs I'd be stuck in if I ever put my mouth too close to a public fountain. My mother carried in her purse a collapsible cup I was to use if I got thirsty.

I played outside when I was little. I leapt and stretched and sashayed for no one but myself. I learned how to make my body beautiful from my family. In winter my grandmother looped artificial pearls over threadbare cashmere sweaters handed down by her employer. She had slacks because she was modern. In summer she wore floral dresses, and enamel bracelets, and shoes that let her polished toes peep out. She was a natural blonde, as was my mother, as am I. I received a beautiful form from them and that was my inheritance. I felt the riches of my mother's glamor and of my grandmother.

A gasoline rainbow glistened in the puddle under my father's new car. Steam billowed out of our bathroom window when my mother showered. She smelled so sweet. But then she died because it all got to be too much.

My fear is that I won't get any more work after this picture. Because of my age. Perhaps Jake will be the last man to want me. I have worked all my life to make my body beautiful enough for the screen and now I'm afraid it's ending. And just when I have stopped running as if pursued by monsters. I now feel time working against me. Even though I barely eat my waist has softened. My hands have a rough texture no matter how much cream I apply.

I don't tell Jake about any of this because I want him to keep his image of me. I used to be the ingénue and now I'm the older woman. I wish I could talk to Lev about it, but he's so rarely home when I call. I wish I could reach him. I know he knows I'm breaking down but he doesn't judge.

Aunt Marie let me hold on to my pain without compelling me to talk about it. Or maybe she did this for herself. It's possible she didn't want to hear what I might say. She had enough of her own struggles. She could fill hours with the telling and retelling of hardships suffered by herself. She had a way of making whatever problem you had feel insufficiently tragic when compared to a story of herself or our ancestors.

Marie had been born with a hair lip. It had been repaired but was still visible as a fine seam between her nostril and mouth. Her mother, my grandmother I guess, had died giving birth to twins when Marie was fourteen. Both the twins also died and that left Marie to take care of my father and his brother and her father as well. Prairie wind whistled through their days. When finally Marie married and had her own child, her husband died all of a sudden in a munitions fire on an army base, leaving her once again to raise yet another boy without assistance or attention.

Maybe because of all the men in the family, Marie treated me like a strange visitor even though I lived with her for years. Girls were not her specialty. Marie kept portraits of the lost and living arranged on a lace doily in the front room. The picture in pride of place was of her son Stanley, a big-eared man in uniform. My cousin I suppose. Stanley floated somewhere in the Pacific with the merchant marines.

Stanley had been away for years. I never met him but all around the house were signs of him. He had a gift from his shipmates during the war, a diploma-like document but instead of a school crest or something official it was covered with hand-painted pretty pinup mermaids and bug-eyed sea monsters. It was to commemorate his first time crossing the equator, Marie told me, and he'd sent it to her for safekeeping. It hung in his empty bedroom that became mine and I never asked to take it down because I knew it would upset her. I liked to spin the globe in his room, running my finger along the raised line that ran around the middle, touching the place in the ocean where my unknown relative might be.

Aunt Marie rarely spoke of my mother, except with a sigh, but she was proud of my father. She often worked into stories how he'd made it into college at sixteen because of his mathematical brilliance. She liked to tell me about how a scientist, who was also an heir to a great manufacturing fortune, had taken my father under his wing, because he'd recognized something special. She included Dr. Colgate in her prayers because of all he'd done for my father, and therefore for all of us.

She made a point of buying both Colgate toothpaste and Murphy Oil Soap even though they weren't the best bargain but because they were manufactured by the family of my father's mentor and she wanted to show her support. I told her my mother said Dr. Colgate was a womanizer who didn't care about family money. Marie said my mother was sometimes too free with her opinions and I shouldn't repeat her mistakes. I was a child, Marie said.

Aunt Marie had worked at the public library, but when I came to live with her she was retired. She was active in the Democratic Party and the Kiwanis Club. My mother always said Marie was a good citizen.

Those years passed in a haze of high school, secrets, bad behavior, and ballet classes at Miss Moreno's School for Dance with other performance-inclined young ladies of Grand Junction.

We practiced in a curtained storefront next to the Thrifty Way. When we were not pas de bourréeing we were listening to Miss Moreno tell us stories of her illustrious family. We heard, more than once, about how her dear mother had defied her family to move all the way from Zaragoza, Spain, to Trenton, New Jersey.

We heard all about how Miss Moreno had belonged to the corps de ballet of the San Francisco Grand Opera. We girls joked that that must have been back in pioneer times because of how stiffly she moved through her demonstrations as the shawl slipped from her bony shoulders. Miss Moreno danced like a puppet made of sticks and wool.

I wasn't that talented, but I stuck with her because I loved the ritual and formality. I also liked the identity I could claim at school. Dancing lengthened my neck. I gleaned tricks of how to appear more beautiful while moving through a room. Those classes gave me a few wrap sweaters I wore until they were riddled with holes. I learned also in those classes, from the other girls, the useful discipline of self-starvation.

I used this all to augment the beauty my mother left me as inheritance. From my father I got some things too, which helped as well. From him I received a gnawing emptiness and a will to work. He gave me long limbs and a precise gaze. I had my mother's radiating core of beauty and sadness. That was my volatile element that wanted to bond with others but couldn't except under the right pressures.

I learned even in high school that all these qualities together had a radioactive kind of effect on people. I could draw in and repel. I knew I had some of what my mother had because of the way men started to look.

Many girls don't want to admit they can recognize their gifts, but I felt mine. I wanted them. I began to take an interest in my appearance because whatever effort I put in bounced around, creating heat and light. I got to be beautiful and that determined the direction my whole life would take.

A girl can be any object. She can be a sandwich half-eaten, or a half a cantaloupe cradling a scoop of cottage cheese. A girl can be a boy's shirt, knotted at the belly button. A girl can be a high arch hidden inside a clean white Ked. A girl can be a ponytail done in a careless fashion. She can be a gesture, a consumable, a style. Aunt Marie didn't notice my teenage allure as long as I didn't wear lipstick in front of her. With lipstick she drew the line. Because of this prohibition I learned how to be subtle. My shoulders were boney and my neck long. I was a human ruffle of recklessness.

If you'd met me then you never would have guessed the pain I had like a hard tumor inside. Or so I liked to think. I was the bubbliest of them all. I thought I was hiding everything in an act of overheated girlhood. What I thought was hidden actually made its own kind of display. I had a blushing wound and it flashed like a beacon for certain kinds. I learned that. I glowed special for those who would do damage. Grown men were my best audience. I could sense how I looked when I walked past them. I felt windblown and light. I suggested with my gait that I could be interfered with, waylaid, fondled and no one would protest, least of all myself. I saw men looking when I was having chocolate floats with my girlfriends.

My dumb signals and baby voice brought me into some frightening situations. Skirting traps as a lark sometimes got me caught. Men from the diner approached me from behind and tapped my shoulder when I was walking home alone. Men from around town stuck their tongues down my throat. They approached me in the movie theater parking lot. There was the neighbor with his big rough hands. There was the carful of boys up in the woods. I don't want to describe any of that. Some of it I liked though. The world got friendly when I got pretty, even though some people had a harsh way of showing their goodwill. I kept myself in one piece and didn't tell my girlfriends, my aunt, or anyone. No one asked. I told myself it didn't hurt.

For years Miss Moreno criticized my missed steps and lazy arms. Still, I wanted to be onstage. I drew badly and owned only a drugstore set of watercolors, but I loved my pictures. I knew art mostly from magazine spreads in *National Geographic* and *Look*. Ancient things like the Parthenon, or the busts of beautiful young men in Rome. Or modern things like Broadway productions and downtown studios, Brando glowering or an expressionist painter caught with a brush mid-flick.

I had no sense of what artists did or what kinds of people they were, but I knew I wanted in. I read that people had to create in new ways now, because of what had happened in the war, the bomb and the Holocaust. Rules had been overturned and many things were possible. Regular joes might be touched by the muse.

While sitting in the bath one evening, learning about the life of Edgar Allan Poe in *Reader's Digest*, I had my revelation. I decided I would not go to junior college as was vaguely planned. I would move to New York instead and be some kind of artist.

To my amazement, Aunt Marie and my father accepted this proposal. Maybe they thought I would be easily overwhelmed. That

I would be battered around by the bustling metropolis for six months or a year and come running back to Colorado with the white flag raised, appropriately chastened.

I don't know where my passion came from, but I decided beforehand I would rather kill myself than return.

I boarded the Royal Gorge Line in Grand Junction one late summer morning.

The long thin train moved us with an impatient clattering. Outside looked bright like a brochure photo. The landscape relaxed from wild geology into well-regulated agriculture. Straight-lined western heartland. Tableaus appeared framed by our windows: white birds flocking in a marsh, cows evenly distributed in a pasture. Fields sprawling out from gray towns. Buildings exposing their back sides to us.

I didn't talk to anyone except the man in the dining car when I bought my Coke. The club car smelled like peanuts and burnt coffee, hair oil and breath long fermented. Groups of men played canasta and drank beer, laughing in different accents and releasing their cards with that satisfying snap.

I was wrapped in my mohair sweater dreaming when a young man sat down beside me. He sported a work shirt and no jacket, thrillingly careless for travel. I felt an attraction but he only glanced at me once. He spent the morning absorbed in a paperback copy of *On the Road*. He scowled as he read and when he grew tired of glowering, he pulled his hat down and hugged himself in half sleep. I spent a while thinking of some spontaneous clever thing to say, but before I could we approached Chicago and everyone began hustling down their bags and string-tied packages. When we disembarked I watched him disappear into the crowd, his book tucked under his arm. He had nothing else, was fancy free.

I arrived in New York City the following day with my bag of precious possessions. Though there was no outer difference except a subtle funk from sitting still for too long, I felt changed, awakened. This was the first time I'd seen anything of the east. From first look I knew it was love.

Aunt Marie had arranged a living situation suitable for a young girl. She and my father agreed if I was to be in the big city I had to be supervised by someone trustworthy. And so, I was entrusted to one Ms. Karla Seidel. Old German friend of my grandmother's.

This was how, at eighteen, I found myself living with yet another widow who saw me as a task. My father paid her for my room and board. I was expected to find some kind of work and some classes to take.

Karla lived not in a cinematic Manhattan apartment as I'd envisioned, but rather in a narrow brick row house in the far-flung Bronx. Coming from out west, you don't have any idea how far you can be from the glamor while still technically being within the municipal boundaries.

Karla's living room hid behind two layers of curtains, one set translucent and the other of thickest brocade that was kept closed to save the couch from fading. On the other side of those curtains, beyond a river and a highway and thousands of buildings you could see the glinting formation of skyscrapers.

I came to my new life with an artificial leather suitcase carefully packed. It held my tight angora sweater and my loose wool one, three blouses, a black skirt and a green one, clean underwear, and a striped pajama set. I had bobby pins and cold cream, lipstick and Shakti deodorant powder all contained in a satin bag. I had a new diary and a silver pen. I had a natural pearl necklace that had been my mother's.

My first job in New York was that of an office assistant in a small factory. Karla got me the job through her social connections.

Over the course of a lunch, it was arranged that I would be taken under the angora-clad wing of Karla's neighbor's daughter, Margaret, or as she preferred, Margot. She told me she liked the name better because it sounded French. She was the first person I met who watched foreign films.

Margot was twenty-one and worked in a factory that produced cheap watches. She told me, though, I should never say "cheap" but rather "economical," "reasonable," or "popularly priced," because that sounded classier. But they were cheap.

Other women spent all day arranging miniature metal springs, pins, and gears onto plastic plates that had sections molded into them. Still other women placed the tiny parts into the backs of the watch faces. But because of Margot and her family I got to work in the office, putting stamps on envelopes and restocking the break room with coffee stirrers and sugar. For this I was paid a wage of $1.10 an hour.

Margot had lived beside Karla since birth. She was friends with a whole gang from the neighborhood. A few attended Bronx Community College while the rest worked. Her group talked too much, all of the time, with great animation. She brought me in, quite generously.

I liked Margot and she liked me too. There was no reason she had to welcome me, socially, but I think she enjoyed having a sidekick from out west. She saw me as kind of exotic and also a blank slate. I didn't know all the social intricacies she was so steeped in.

Right off the bat Margot told me her big secret. She was having a romance with this man Glenn Elloway, but her mother didn't know. He was not from the neighborhood and didn't attend church. They'd met when he was repairing a machine in the factory. She said Glenn rooted for the Yankees, had a lingering injury from when he was in Manila, and loved her passionately. At first sight, he said. Glenn had money to take Margot out and she liked that. He was a real man and wanted to get married but she was holding off because she hadn't decided yet. Maybe she wanted to travel and do something with her life. I promised to keep her confidence.

With all the other people I met Margot slipped me fragments of the bigger pictures, family losses and aches, fights and talents that were known. Daniel was off in the head since his mother died. Just watch out because he gets mad easily. Betty was sweet but fragile; Anne Marie, on the other hand, was a barrel of laughs. Alan, Mike, and Marie were siblings, Mikey and Nicky best friends. And then there was Jack and Elizabeth, Bobby, Robert and John Jr. and Susan and Candy.

These boys and girls shared names with each other as if there was a shortage. Variations also belonged to parents and relatives near and distant. There was a great need for modifiers, nicknames, or the use of last names to know who was meant but I had to grab for clues and nod when a story was in full swing. There were enough romances and flirtations and dalliances to make it feel like I had dropped into a long running soap opera.

One time Margot took me along to a party in the city with people Glenn knew. Glenn drove aggressively and played the radio loud. She and I spent the party laughing it up with a couple who were about to move to California. They kept refilling our cups with wine. They met while studying acting and told me all about it. The girl said the class they took was full of snobs but you could still learn a boatload about your emotions.

Margot spent the whole ride home apologizing to Glenn for not paying him enough attention. He sulked and brooded and criticized. I felt like their silent child, pressing my head against the window and observing the cream-colored full moon playing peekaboo in the gaps between buildings, wishing more than anything to be free of their caustic imitation adulthood.

Margot and her friends wore beautiful colors in a loose style. They were stick thin; debonair in too-big trousers handed down from an older brother. Somehow sexy in a Peter Pan collar. They could cinch a belt and roll a sleeve like nobody. We leaned on John's car, hung around making jokes in the park at night.

They knew all these dances I'd never heard of before and taught me the steps. I got good at the weight shifts and hip swings, forgetting easily the formality Miss Moreno had thumped into us ballet students. This dancing offered real velocity and torque with sexual tension. The boys had so much energy and could swing you around bodily. It was so very fun because it was clear they could give a shit—pardon my French—if we lived or died. God help all the girls in the arms of sweet boys with homicidal moods.

One April day when the trees were still hard and dull but the air was newly soft and moist, Margot and I sat outside to eat our bag lunches. I could feel something was amiss. Like she wanted to talk about something without others overhearing. Her skin was all puffed-up under a heavy coat of makeup. She fiddled with a paper coffee cup and made me take her Stella D'oro cookies. She wasn't hungry, she swore. I accepted to be nice, waiting for the unspoken to make itself plain.

Glenn and I are getting married, she blurted out. We decided over the weekend.

I was tactless and incredulous. Glenn was as sullen as Margot was bright. I asked what had become of her dreams of singing in nightclubs, Mediterranean cafés, adventuresome men who had sailboats and knew about Caribbean coves. She had put these visions in my head. I pushed too far and asked about Glenn's black moods.

You don't have to drag Glenn's name through the mud, she said. He's going to be my husband. Glenn's uncle promised a good job for him up in Kingston. Glenn was so technically minded and the city had gotten so dirty. Glenn promised Margot their own place with a fenced-in yard and a new puppy to run circles in it.

He warned me that you were a jealous person and now I see what he was talking about. I was stung. If that's how she wanted to be, I thought, have at it. We went back into work and didn't walk home together as usual. Glenn came and got her in his car.

Karla already knew all about Margot's happy news by the time I returned home that evening. Isn't it nuts, I asked. Isn't it a huge mistake? Karla shook her head and stayed mum.

At the wedding Margot cried at the altar. We were supposed to think they were tears of happiness. Not so long after, that fall I guess it was, Margot sent me a note with a photo of her new baby daughter. I wrote a postcard back saying how cute the baby was but I never heard anything more.

White clouds floated in the cool blue sky above the green park. I had told the watch factory I was sick. But really I couldn't face it anymore. I was heading toward the Metropolitan Museum, tasting that particular sweetness that comes from roaming around on a beautiful day when you're supposed to be at work.

I had on that day one of my rather disappointing Colorado skirts. It was clean and serviceable and I couldn't bring myself to get rid of it. Shame over waste was a lesson I had learned well from Marie. While the skirt was dowdy my cheekbones were high and properly blushed. My posture was good and I had on my nicest accessories as protection. I wore my idiocy boldly. I was in desperate need of revelation and I was prepared to do anything to get it.

I climbed the stone stairs, perfumed and eager. I paid the fee and held the paper map before me. There was an exhibition of Primitive Art with sculptures of wood. There was a large and special exhibit of American paintings and sculptures with Sargent and Graves and Hopper northeast of the Arms and Armor Hall. And if I didn't care for those, French decorative arts beckoned with flounces and pastels and small fluffy dogs.

While looking I felt myself being looked at. A young man appeared beside me. With a simple hello I was lost. He said these smooth lines made him think of Saarinen. The best designer, he said. Did I know him? I did not. He complimented the scarf I had tied over my hair. It was one of my mother's, genuine silk with a burnt umber and aquamarine pattern. We ended up talking quietly as we walked from one gallery to the next. I pictured myself in the eyes of the women in bouclé suits. They might imagine we were a couple.

He asked if I would like to get a coffee. But I don't even know your name. He said Ivan, now will you come to coffee? He was so gentle in his crisp suit and pretty tie. What could it hurt? And I said all right as long as it wasn't too far. I felt like a shaken-up bottle of Coke. Maybe this is how you fall in love, I thought.

I expected a lunch counter or a diner, but he brought me to a hushed hotel restaurant. The tables were draped in white and nestled into half-circle dark red booths. We were led to a corner. The place was well past a meal rush, after lunch and a while to dinner, pleasantly dim and cool. He ordered us coffee and two slices of a European kind of cake.

Something was happening. He had a suave plan and this was the first time a man had had one of those for me. I let myself drift. He asked questions and pouted slightly when I explained about Karla, and Kingsbridge, and Colorado. He stretched out the sounds of the place. He asked me about it. I told him it was where a lot of mines were. It's where they dug up coal and copper, vanadium, and uranium. All the men were ranchers and miners. I assumed everyone would know to roll their eyes at such figures, as I did. How funny you come from there, I've never met a western girl, he sighed.

He said he worked at his father's office part-time. The rest of his time he devoted to classes. When I asked what kind he said all sorts. He'd been studying piano since childhood but was now expanding his interests, figure drawing at the Art Students League, acting at a studio. One of his arms rested on the leather seat back behind me. He had the look of Dirk Bogarde at a certain angle and I told him so. He rolled his eyes. I tingled.

My fork lifted and fell as I took smaller and smaller bites of cake trying to make its richness last.

The waiter offered more coffee and Ivan accepted on our behalf. As the waiter disappeared around a corner Ivan scooted closer. He moved his arm from behind my neck to down right beside my leg. May I show you my notebook? he asked. I sensed there was more.

I think you're gorgeous, Ivan said. And maybe you're a bit wilder than you let on? His hand came to rest on my thigh, under the table, hidden by the tablecloth. I knew completely I was supposed to recoil, scandalized and chaste, but I was too curious for that. Are you, he asked. I replied, maybe. Maybe meant yes. I wanted to know how far things could go in public with a stranger who looked so buttoned up.

Are you happy with this, he asked as his hand whispered up my thigh. Shall we chat some more? I could stay all afternoon, I said.

Ivan managed to keep up his end of friendly banter as his hand, hidden beneath the table, moved under the edge of my skirt. I acted as if I didn't feel like shuddering. His fingers brushed up and up before gently finding my panties' edge.

His fingers pushed inside me as the rest of his body appeared polite, disinterested even. We leaned our heads close over his notebook while he moved his hand subtly but with increasing intensity between my legs. I had had something like this happen at a movie theater once, but that was hard and clumsy, whereas this was practiced, silky. He searched and fluttered with a musical rhythm.

I met some people at a party once who took acting classes. Have you been in any plays, I asked. Can just anyone go study?

We were like swans gliding. Serene above the surface while down below there was a great effort. Look at me, he said. Look in my eyes. Pretend you're calm. Him saying that made me more excited.

I inched closer to what I was supposed to resist. Does that feel good? he asked. Yes, it's so nice, I breathed. Would you mind very much saying my name? Oh Ivan, I said. He made the faintest nod. I felt a decisive turn, and shuddered.

After a moment of pleased stillness, he removed his hand and wiped it with a cloth napkin. We continued pretending nothing had happened. I smoothed my skirt back over my knees.

The waiter returned with a bill that Ivan paid with a smile.

Ivan walked me to the subway, giving careful advice on maintaining my welfare underground. He inquired about stops and corresponding bus lines and I showed him the index card I had with the route written out. At the station he kissed both my cheeks farewell like they did in European movies. No man had ever done that to me before.

———

Once upon a time, the Eldorado Hotel marked the northern edge of the town. It had been a grand place when it was built during a silver boom. It was decorated in a plush European style and had a dining hall with a menu of steaks and champagne, canned peaches and whipped cream. It had a proscenium theater that could seat a healthy crowd. The voices of traveling operetta singers and orators once echoed through this space that now belonged to a colony of bats.

Now the town of Commodore, Colorado, has only a handful of functioning buildings. They are arranged along a single strip of road with steep hills climbing up behind them. We are in a valley, but also high up. You can tell by how hard you have to breathe with a simple stroll, and by how easily everyone gets drunk.

Though the town of Commodore is a husk of its former self, it isn't exactly uninhabited. It has a few bare-bones businesses and the whiff of things to come.

There is the Owl Bar, which hangs on because of the prodigious thirst of loggers, truckers, and adventuring Hells Angels. The gas station general store services the needs of families with vacation cabins farther on, selling precut firewood bundles and marshmallows, cheap fishing rods and a variety of garishly colored hand-tied flies. It's good trout fishing, they say.

The Eldorado Hotel, where we are installed, is long defunct and set to be torn down come spring. There is talk of a resort, investments from Denver or Dallas. Someone told our director this town could be the next Sun Valley or Vail. The high rollers, the beautiful people could come here to ski and be seen. Our film would herald in a new era in Mineral County, or so the whispers went.

The producers were able to rent the Eldorado for a song. We were told the crew could do whatever they wished: track mud through the halls, knock down a wall. Nothing was precious. I think this has benefited the look of the film. Our shots glow with age. You can see the patina of decay in the rushes. All the dust gives our scenes a tintype, antique feel.

In terms of our daily life though, all this history is a different matter. Everything in our living quarters is rotten, broken, or both. The floorboards bow beneath the weight of our feet. I hug the walls because the edges feel more solid than the center. I don't want to break an ankle on some decomposing step.

Only a few bathrooms in the hotel are functional. We are ten to a toilet on a good day. You can imagine the smells of so many tromping in, dropping trousers and lifting skirts to expel our anxious gassy waste. Hour upon hour.

The men have taken to our circumstances easily. They revel in the collective rusticism. They are growing beards to get into character, pissing en plein air and bathing in the creek, just to show off. We women trade in sprays, mists, and scented oils. We are advocating for the building of a temporary bathhouse of some kind. I argue to Tony it might be incorporated into the story somehow.

I remind myself that making art means trade-offs and balancing acts. I don't always know why that's the case but it is. If I wasn't here it would be another actress in my place. You adapt but also hold your nose.

I'm figuring out how to fix my makeup by lamplight and becoming adept at washing from a basin. At the end of each night, I air my clothes out and sprinkle them with rose-scented powder. Jake smells sweaty and fresh at the same time. I forget New York and how clean I was. My hair has gotten quite disheveled already and my only option is to brush it out like I'm a horse or a Victorian lady.

Sometimes when I am too cold or drunk to face the travails of the long hall and the dank bathroom, I hang my bare ass out the window and pee down the wall.

It's embarrassing that I first went to an acting class in hopes of meeting a man who'd touched me beneath a restaurant table, but it was my motivation. Sex is such an excellent motivator, maybe the best when you're young.

When I told Jake the story of the museum encounter, he laughed. It's not the kind of origin story you tell just anyone, but another actor will understand. How many of us have stumbled into a life of acting while looking for one with an erotic charge?

When I remember Ms. Auger I think of all the details that led to her. She was not only a person but a place in time, a practice, a state of being. What she created formed me. It no longer exists. I long for it still.

You had to climb five shabby flights to get to Ms. Mira Auger's acting studio. Once you'd puffed your way up, you came onto a landing with a window. Many moths met their end in the space between screen and glass and no one had ever cleaned out these dust-soft carcasses. The smell of exhaust and the sounds of traffic came through that closed window. Muffled voices and machine noise rose through the floorboards and floated around the stairwell. Sometimes there was singing from the voice teacher's studio on a lower floor.

Beside the door was a tall wooden shelf. Here you were supposed to leave street shoes and put on in their stead the clean tennis or soft ballet shoes you had brought for stage work. Needing special shoes was one of the first lessons you got when you started studying with Mira.

I spent a lot of time in that narrow strip of real estate, alone or with my fellow students. It was the place to catch your breath or smooth your hair, remind yourself one last time of your lines and motivation. It was the place to work yourself up into the proper state to withstand the X-ray gaze of a true theater artist.

We students were in charge of preparing the studio each day before our teacher's arrival. We took turns sweeping, arranging the chairs, preparing the tea, and boiling water for the samovar. Ms. Auger's tea preferences were so particular as to become a password in the theater world. To know about the strength of the Darjeeling was to show you really belonged.

Mira was the last person to arrive, or at least that was how it was supposed to go. Entering after Ms. Auger was so embarrassing that only a few masochists ever dared. The first time Richie arrived late she ignored him. The second time she forbade him to participate and the third time he was banned from our group for a month. He crawled back into her good graces by bringing her imported French cookies and a groveling apology.

Even with or maybe because of this misbehavior, Richie was one of Ms. Auger's favorites, something I wished desperately to be. The boys always got away with more.

Mira was a woman used to being waited for, anticipated. She arrived, she settled, she graced us with the glow of herself. She communicated in her bearing a long history of rigorous training and overheated adoration. She could withstand the pressure of many eyes bearing down on her, the desire of a crowd.

When Mira arrived we all turned our faces in gratitude, like sunflowers toward the glowing east.

She was old when I studied with her, I'm not sure how, but if I had to guess I'd say sixty-five. Ms. Auger had been a specific kind of beauty that had more to do with charisma than an undeniable physical look. Or maybe hers was an old-fashioned kind of beauty that no longer meant the same in our age of photoplay spreads. She dressed in turtlenecks and slacks, light blouses and long pendants.

She carried, some days, a cane, all the better to beat on the floor when she wanted to make a memorable point. She kept her mouth uncolored but drew lines of kohl around her large eyes. Her skin was powdery fine and it lay delicately over the skull beneath. Like silk over a marble ball. Ms. Auger's voice could be soft or it could fill the room. She could seem quite gentle and ladylike. Her eyelashes fluttered freely but the gaze behind them was very penetrating. Those eyes had taken in more scenes than we young disciples could comprehend.

She described steamship ballrooms and coffee shops in Tangiers, Hamburg as it once was, all pastel reflections and needle fine spires. She told us all about the brazen assassination she had witnessed one day on a street corner in Budapest. She'd seen with her big expressive eyes blood mix with rainwater as it ran into a storm drain.

And when it came to the arts, the anecdotes became thicker with names and mystery. She had seen Jessner's production of Hamlet in peacetime Berlin and Schoenberg play the piano in wartime Los Angeles. Josef von Sternberg adored her. She'd been Nora and Irina onstage of course, but she had also appeared on an episode of *Death Valley Days* because she was no snob. An actor had to work. She spoke of all this airily, as if we all knew what she meant.

Her accent was impossible to pin down, emerging out of a place somewhere between Moscow and Santa Monica. She could make herself sound like a thousand different women.

When we were shooting *Abend—Nacht—Morgen*, she said, that was the first time I really controlled my instrument. With Murnau I learned how to make artifice and strangeness into a natural-sounding tone. Simply thinking as a character can communicate more sometimes than any amount of acting. You must work out what is going through your character's mind at each moment. Then you must let it flow through you organically. Onstage you must use your whole body but on film it is better to think as your character. Keep it close on camera. Wear your characters' thoughts like a perfume.

She made us feel like heaps of raw material, as doughy as babies. It was not only her age but the depth of her experience that put us to shame. She said Americans were all children but that's why she loved us, because we were brash and sometimes teachable. I hoped I was.

The *I*, my little self, dissolved as soon as it hit the hot liquid of art. If you have never fallen under the spell of a discipline you will not appreciate the power of belonging it brings. I was so lonely that the rapturous feeling of being seen by a teacher was almost too much.

Before Mira I was afraid I might be dumb, maybe only useful as an assistant at the watch factory office. But she swept away my fears and my memories of tedious high school English class. She made me love Shakespeare, Chekhov, and Brecht. Then of course there were the Americans, like O'Neill, Sinclair, and Hansberry, who we admired, but she helped us get to the heart of why they were great, what they were talking about. She made us all understand. We felt the words because of her. And because this process of understanding unfolded collectively, the pleasure was multiplied.

She convinced us we could understand because they were writing about seducers and those who wanted to be seduced, idiots and depressives, connivers and romantics. We came to understand because she believed we could.

Even though Mira was dedicated to the text, we always began with the body. We warmed up our muscles. We sang and chanted vocal exercises. We relearned our bodies and began to talk about them not as selves but as instruments or tools.

Like in ballet class, the studio was a place where everyday rules of movement were upended, only here the method was much more thrilling and opaque. We'd lie on the floor humming and ha-ha-ing. From that we'd progress to crawling and slithering. With knuckle dragging we'd cross the room in slow motion. Other times we'd whip the walls madly with our loose, long hair. All was possible. We were sometimes conjuring babies and sometimes wild animals.

And though we kept to the rules of classroom cleanliness, the floors were mopped with dirty water and had been waxed so many times that a film transferred onto us no matter what. Your practice shoes and your socks, your palms and the knees of your pants were grimy by the end of the class. Getting messed up was a part of the process.

After the physical stuff we ran through difficult scenes. We all had a sob story and could tell it. We could cry on command but had no interest in self-pity. Sometimes we simulated pain for comic potential.

In the stifling heat of summer, we'd strip down to as close to indecent as possible. Undershirts and shorts, bare legs and glistening backs of necks. We spritzed Florida water down our blouses and under our armpits. There was more acting to do and all we wanted was to make Mira happy. We were jumping out of our skins with desiring nerves. We'd think of new human dramas to try. Why don't you pull down my zipper onstage. Trespass on me. It will make the scene better. Let's try it.

We watched one another and offered feedback when Mira gave us permission. Mostly though, she was the one who judged.

After it was all over we'd descend the stairs, loose and spent. We were desperate for cigarettes since Ms. Auger forbade smoking in the studio. We came out of session looking like artsy coal miners or maybe performers in a musical about orphans, smudged and long-limbed. We wiped the sweat from our brows with the backs of our hands. The fresh dirty air of the street touched us inappropriately and we'd sigh. It was heaven. Talking through what had happened we'd share an orange, distributing segments evenly between us. Someone had a bag of sunflower seeds and a bottle of pep pills if we wanted to keep going. We did, of course.

———

It's amazing how much you forget as you age and who you remember. It's astounding to see who survives and who falls. That alone makes aging interesting, just the story arcs alone are quite something. There were many of us but now I can only remember physical details of some, names of others.

When not rehearsing or memorizing or reading, we made money however we could. Mira showed us how our lives could be a place of study to make us better actors. We sold shoes and served breakfast specials. Then afterward we'd write notes about how the customers moved and spoke. We cleaned floors and typed and filed while marveling at the spontaneous choreography of labor. Theater made life itself addictive. We picked up other people's grocery orders, sold fancy pens, and pantyhose, and imported sturgeon roe at a speciality store. We did whatever was needed so that we could keep paying dues at Ms. Auger's studio.

We discussed war, wars. We discussed atomic weapons and the inspirational Fidel Castro. We loved to exclaim and shake out the crispness of that day's newspaper. We'd read to each other but we were foolish when it came to specifics. We wanted to make statements from the stage. We cared a lot or else maybe we were frivolous and only performing politics. We loved art more than we cared for the politics of the world. Acting was the only thing we committed to with our whole selves.

We did not sleep, we collapsed. We rose. We gathered together like a bouquet of flowers. Did we eat if we were not piled together in diner booths? Doubtful. I can't remember the taste of food in that time, only that we must have had something to stay alive.

Some of Ms. Auger's acting students had perfect skin while others among us were that kind of unique ugly that wraps around to become a new kind of alluring.

Steven was my favorite. I thought he was the most beautiful man and moving actor among us. He was from Tennessee and liked boys. He supported himself as the assistant to a gentleman who belonged to some grand uptown family. Steven helped the man buy art from poor bohemians.

I went to movies with Steven and after he'd rhapsodize about framing and timing, themes and silences. I began to understand what made some directors better than others, at least according to Steven's philosophy. I learned about tracking shots when we saw *Touch of Evil*. We talked about the cinematography but also about the bikers in their black leather and what harm they did to Janet Leigh in the scene that happened off-screen.

Richie, who was Mira's golden boy, was a Catholic pervert with bedroom eyes. He liked to grope all the women when we were waiting behind the curtains and I secretly enjoyed it. During smoke breaks he talked about girlfriend troubles while I swooned.

Years later, after I lost track of him, Suzanna told me he committed suicide. She never heard the reason why.

Though I had thought the group was special and inseparable, nothing much lasted. We disintegrated. Suzanna is the only friend I've managed to keep from that time.

She was a divorcée and at twenty-five she was older and more urbane than the rest of us. She'd lived in Mexico City and had silver and turquoise jewelry and striped blankets over her furniture to prove it. Suzanna was the first person to show me how artists really lived, in real present life. I trusted her taste in all things. I confided in her about my mother and her beautiful problems. She said that's how I got my specialness.

Suzanna's apartment on Perry Street had spider plants and stained-glass decorations. I sometimes slept there when I couldn't face the train back to Karla's. I remember hearing Nina Simone for the first time while lying on her floor. One among so many revelations of that time. I had my head resting on Suzanna's hip while Steven and Richie lay on either side of us. We listened to the record all the way through and when it was over we did it again. Her singular voice made me believe not just that another world was possible, but that it was close enough to touch.

In my time under the spell of Ms. Auger I behaved with super-human control, romantically speaking. Though we touched and kissed one another in all manner of configurations onstage, I never got mixed up with my fellow actors in life. It seemed incestuous. I wanted my unfixed vitality to remain an open channel. Acting was my way to stay within a magic net. I didn't want to damage it by getting stuck on one point of love, disappointment, or jealousy. I remembered what true love had done to Margot.

Still, I went out sometimes, on the sly. I liked men who could afford tickets and gifts without thinking about it. I switched between a few who took me to films and plays, dinners in clattering restaurants, and drinks in narrow bars with red-tinted light. I did some making out, getting felt up in the backs of cabs. I went as far as hand jobs and fingering but then I'd wriggle away. I always kept myself partially dressed. I had a layer of distrust clinging beneath my clothes. It kept me separated. Whenever one man got too tired of me for not putting out, I'd find another willing to go through the whole process because I was slim and flirtatious.

At the end of these evenings, I always made my way back to the Bronx.

In my narrow room with its pink wallpaper, I'd wipe away whatever smells that still clung to me from out there. Under the light of the wobbly lamp with its pleated shade I'd study my precious objects. My pair of black leather heels stood beside my pink flats with the bow. I'd stuck to the wall pictures of places I wanted to see. A Gothic church and a misty grove, a technicolor seascape, and an embellished old apartment building with a stack of balconies overlooking a bustling piazza.

My hair ribbons draped over the vanity mirror, while my diary, my pencils and eyelash curler and Pond's cream sat waiting for me. The purse that had accompanied me out into the wilds of the world and had witnessed what I had and had not done hung off the door-knob. My purse's little clasp was locked tight. The bag concealed within itself loose coins, a compact and a lipstick, a Samuel French play script, and a book of matches with a man's office phone number written on the inside flap.

In the mirror I saw that ineffable feminine glow. I'd brush my hair and pat my skin with rosewater. If I turned my head just so, I was beautiful like my mother. My eyes were large and set wide, my hair the blond like people wanted. My starvation and pills kept my neck and collarbones fragile. What could all this be worth? A life on the stage? A series of destinations? I was bent on finding out. How full of bravado I was. How like an individual I felt in my private night moments.

On a May morning in my twenty-first year, I packed my suitcase. I was going away for the entire summer. I had a train ticket to Old Lyme, Connecticut, the following morning because I had gotten a job at a summer theater. It was a modest, workaday acting job, but it was still professional and I would get to live by the sea. I was over the moon.

Suzanna was, I think, the only one from Ms. Auger's class who was really happy for me. Others were jealous, even though some had gotten small off-Broadway parts and the like. We were all making our way but I guess I got to leave town and that seemed like more than I deserved. I would get room and board.

In front of everyone, Mira announced my success, practically setting me up for resentment. As she spoke I got hot all over. Richie grinned too wide. One girl conscientiously studied the ceiling. On the street after class the same girl said good luck in the way that sounds like drop dead. Mira, all concern, used me as an example, a lesson for everyone else. She said I might feel disappointed with both the quality of the productions and my roles. Summer stock was for sun-drunk vacationers after all. But, she sighed, I should work as hard as ever, as even a few lines can shine if delivered the right way. In an instant change of feeling, I couldn't wait to leave Mira and this school I'd so loved.

Into cotton bags I nested my black heels, my pink flats, and a pair of fresh white tennis shoes for rehearsals. I piled up three skirts and two pairs of pedal pushers; two sweater sets and blouses with sleeves and without; scarves for neck or hair or waist as decoration. I packed my leotards and tights and my blue jeans. I tied up my bad bras and my good ones with new underwear Karla had bought me; I packed my diary, my lip and eye pencils, my eyelash curler, and my bottle of Coty L'Aimant. The perfume smelled clean to me, and that was what I wanted. Nothing makes a woman more feminine to a man, said the advertisement in *Vogue*.

The smell of real lilacs came and went in the air. Karla's back garden was full of them. Most of the year they were disappointing scraggly green bushes, but for these few weeks they provided pure magic. I hummed to myself and I added to my pile my eyelet top and favorite pink and yellow shift.

Karla came to my doorway bearing a bottle of aspirin and one of antacids. They might not be glamorous, she said, but you'll be thankful you have them. She fiddled with the bottles and shook her head at the state of my room. Don't leave it like this, she said. I sensed she wanted to tell me something more. I hated mushy advice and faux mothering.

Don't get pregnant, Karla said plainly, that's all I ask. She placed the pill bottles on my dresser and went to make sandwiches. I thought to myself how absurd the older generation could be.

The Old Lyme Playhouse was a red barn in the middle of a green field. It was set back from the road, with a long driveway that led to a parking lot of fine white gravel. These tiny rocks jumped into my shoes all summer, causing a ritual of limping and stork-legged shoe shaking. Whenever there was a show on, pastel cars filled the lot like eggs beside the big hen of the barn.

The Playhouse put on eight shows a week and was run by a couple named Martin and Minty Satterlee. Minty belonged to a fortune of some kind. I came to understand that the area was chockablock with this sort, but at the start of my summer I was innocent about how the rich behaved. She was the decision maker.

Despite or perhaps because of her family, Minty was a stingy boss. For the whole summer I was paid one hundred and fifty dollars, plus room and board. I was the worst paid but the others didn't fare so much better. I made more over a couple weeks at the watch factory. Our food and lodgings were laughable, that summer I survived on unbuttered English muffins and thin coffee, celery sticks and apples at lunch, and overcooked casseroles at dinner.

Minty said we were using the tissue in the camp bathroom with wanton abandon. We spent our pay on cigarettes and alcohol. But it didn't matter. None of it did. I would have slept in the grass and paid them to act.

The only generous meal they served us was when we first arrived as a welcome. That was the day Martin and Minty's friends were there too, come to survey the artists and drink juleps. That day looked like a *Better Homes and Gardens* spread. Vases of flowers and a white tent, glossy mussels and corn, baby potatoes and oily sausages piled on trays. I was dazzled into thinking the whole summer would be one big celebration. At that party my body felt perfectly relaxed.

How many small disasters develop out of a young woman's expectations? Even asking the question feels stupid. Young women skirt disaster or succumb to it. Those are the options. That's regular. It's hardly a story except when you're the woman and then it's everything. And on the disaster side, there are so many flavors and shades it's easy to lose track.

I have never been too clear on desire. It's like looking. Does the thing reach out to my eyes or do my eyes envelop what I see? Do I want to be liked by another or to be like them?

It's like this. A girl sees a man doing something and she wants to do what he does. He smiles. Wearing a rumpled uniform, he strides toward a plane, readying himself to lift into the clouds. A woman runs to catch up, to throw herself into his arms because, though she is afraid for him, he is brave. Because of the way things are in society, I could not see a way to do what the man does, with his free swagger and panache, bravery, and sense of liberty. Because his way of being felt inaccessible to me I recognized the next best thing was to embrace this kind of charming man. She presses herself to him in the hopes that his way of life will rub off on her. She kisses. She inhales his breath not because it is sweet but because she hopes it will animate her body as it does his.

I have lost years of myself in this confusion. I did not know the difference between wanting a man to want me, and wanting to do what he did. When I was young, I slept with men because I wanted to be them, more than I wanted to be with them. And what was worse is the men I chose were themselves mimics, shadows, pretenders.

It's bad luck to fall for actors and make yourself their audience, but that's what I've done, time and again.

I'll call the Old Lyme lead actor Vince because it's like the word "convince" and he was good at that. That wasn't his name but what's the point of revealing his real one? You've probably seen him in movies, though he was never quite a star. I don't say his name because he has a wife and kids, because saying his real name would pin it all down and that's not something I care to do.

Mr. Convince had thick wavy hair and a permanent upturn at one corner of his mouth, like a smirk. A toothpick or dangling cigarette belonged there. He looked as if he was always thinking of a private joke. He looked good in his broad-chested body. He shrugged good. He sighed and slouched and sang well. When you'd ask for a light for your cigarette he'd lean in and whisper something into your ear, nothing dirty, but maybe just bordering. He looked like Paul Newman's brother if you were drunk and he was more than willing to buy you enough drinks to make that so.

He'd had some success on Broadway. Because of that he had starring roles in two of the four plays we were doing that summer in Old Lyme. On *Importance of Being Earnest* nights, he became John "Jack" Worthing. But the character too was a divided pretender. Jack became Earnest in the country. When he was Vince playing Jack pretending to be Earnest his whole body changed, he became slim and quick with a green flower on his fine gray lapel.

On *View from the Bridge* nights, he became Eddie, who was wide and angry. A city accent flew out of him. He prowled the stage in his faded work shirt, doomed from the start. On Eddie nights he would kiss me roughly and real in front of the whole audience. When we'd rehearsed it he'd been respectful but in production he invented variations, a shoulder grab, a slip of tongue even though the director said not to. My character had to break away, horrified, for onstage I was his niece and it was all too strange and incestuous, but inside myself I loved it and he seemed to as well, at least for a while.

When I asked about how he prepared for these two different performances, how he kept his roles separate, he laughed and said the costumes helped. I hope you don't go in for method, he said with a wag of his finger. It will get you all twisted. Know your lines, put on your clothes, and imagine you're a different person, he advised. Keep it simple. He said he dove into whatever night it was. He didn't like to talk about acting, said he wanted to forget all the studying he'd done.

Vince and I gravitated toward one another. We'd find ourselves side by side while getting a coffee from the carafe. There were times in corners, before rehearsal, and during breaks. He'd brush against me in the narrow hall to the dressing rooms and let himself linger. When we'd all be walking back to the gender-separated cabins where we actors slept as if we were kids in summer camp, Vince would sing out, Irene goodnight, I'll see you in my dreams. And the other actresses would *tsk-tsk* him, but with obvious affection.

One Sunday after a matinee he asked if anyone wanted to go swimming and I was the only one to say yes. He was the door. I pushed gently and he swung open.

It was really too cool for the beach. A rainstorm had swept through the night before, ridding the air of the usual humidity. The sun was setting and the water was freezing but we leapt in anyway. I shrieked and he laughed.

All wet on the sand I turned from white to blue. He lent me his flannel shirt and rubbed both my arms with a violent up-and-down motion. Get the blood moving. He gave me a swig from his flask and he drank some beers he'd brought. The sun's last rays slanted across the water. The cool wind dried his hair. Insects whirred in the beach grass. The warm light and blue shadows reminded me of an instance in childhood, but I could not get my mind around the specifics.

While lounging on one elbow, Mr. Convince confided with a sigh that he and his wife were practically divorced. He complimented my swimsuit. I giggled. I didn't pull away when he stroked my thigh. I let my knees fall apart like that time after the museum. This, I thought, was another gap in my official life. He slipped his hands under the elastic edges of my bikini as we kissed. He squeezed my breasts. This doesn't count, I thought.

We took a drive to the next town over where he bought me a lobster roll, and then a spumoni, and then, before driving back to the theater, we climbed into the backseat of his silver Chevrolet Delray. I wanted to do this since I first laid eyes on you, he sighed. We kissed and stroked until I was delirious and said yes to everything.

When my period was supposed to come, it didn't. I'd always been as dependable as a wall calendar, every twenty-eight days with little variation. I hardly thought about my insides because they worked so well. I tracked myself to know what to expect so I wouldn't make stains. Each day of the month that I bled I drew a circle on the corner of the dated box. For around seven days each month, beneath the photograph of baby rabbits in a field of pink flowers or the image of kittens tangled in balls of yarn, I drew my circles, and then I'd go back to normal.

But that July, when I should have been making my marks beneath the photo of retriever puppies surrounded by Independence Day streamers, there was nothing except a sick, heavy feeling inside. Swollen sensations flitted at the edge of my awareness as the unmarked days piled up.

To tempt my bloated insides, I put on my new white shorts, and then the next day my favorite skirt that was light and covered in a strawberry print. It would show everything. I took a swim, fluttering my legs. When I lay face down on the towel, I pressed my fists into my belly as hard as I could.

Vince and I had done nothing after that night in the Delray. I'd tried and failed to catch his eye. He lavished his attention on everyone else but me, Minty and Martin, the stage manager, the other actors, and even the usherettes. I moped on my bed and read a stack of plays and magazines borrowed from the stage manager, who was only a few years older than me but knew more about the world.

On Sunday after our matinee Vince announced to those assembled that he was heading into the city to visit his wife. He'd be back in time for Tuesday's performance and would anyone like a ride? The woman who played Lady Bracknell and the man who played Mike jumped at the chance. They slid into that car all jokes and chatter, Vince tooting his horn as they pulled out of the drive.

I scurried away to flop face down on my bed. I felt suffocated within my skin. Nothing happened. The sun set on another humid green day.

———

More days passed. I couldn't take it. I confided in Kitty, the stage manager. I told her the whole thing through tears that rose up from a deeply drilled well. I blubbered how I'd seen Vince as a door that led to another life. Oh, honey. She sighed. We all saw him toying with you, she said. It made me ill to know how obvious it had been.

Once I'd emptied myself, Kitty got down to specifics. She gave instructions to survive. First, I'd need a doctor to confirm. I needed to wear a ring on my wedding finger when I went to the office. She had one in the costume jewelry bin. Don't say too much about your husband. Once you've got the results Vince will have to take you somewhere. He would have to pay, she said. Make him do the legwork. If he doesn't go along, I'll threaten to tell his wife. You better believe I'll do it too, she added.

After a few attempts of catching him in a discreet corner I finally had to pin Vince down in the parking lot. He made a big show of offering me a ride to town, so that people wouldn't be suspicious at us talking. It was as if he were afraid of me.

In the car at first he acted out a friendly easygoing scene, but it fell apart when I stuttered about how I was late. Each day the trouble grew heavier, bloodier, inside. I didn't say that but he grasped what had happened. I realized then he wasn't as talented as I'd believed him to be at the start of the summer. He knew his lines but his delivery was wooden. He raked his hand through his hair and even kind of knocked his skull with his fist. When he spoke all that came out was a puff of cigarette breath. Some nonsense.

Vince was saying something or other about how this had all been a mistake. He'd never meant for it to go like this. I was so pretty; he'd gotten carried away. He said he'd figure it out. Sit tight kid, he consoled with a pat to the shoulder. I could have died.

At the appointed hour Vince dropped me off at a diner in New Haven. It was a Monday so we were free from the theater. He left me and said he'd be back there to pick me up when the deed was done. I didn't know how long that was supposed to be. I sat down, ordered, then read something in my *New Yorker* magazine. There have been meetings at the Palais des Nations in Geneva, many meetings about nuclear testing. Last year the U.S. was dragging its feet but now it is the Russians who are dragging theirs. The feet of nations were tucked beneath conference tables in hard black dress shoes. They tapped across marble floors in tight groups. They were always well polished.

At my side on the booth cushion sat my big summer purse. It contained a sanitary belt, a change of underwear, and a dark skirt, in case. My bag contained my pocketbook and that held a white envelope with a hundred dollars inside. I kept patting the side to make sure the money remained there. When Vince had handed over the envelope, he'd had a pained look. Be careful with this and give it to the man only after he's finished.

I felt the waitress looking at me. She came over to say her shift was ending and did I want anything before settling up. I apologized for taking so long. I was fine. Waiting for my ride.

Thank you, ma'am. I spun the last sips to make my tepid coffee more appealing.

Finally, my ride did arrive. A strange man came up from behind and tapped my shoulder. I flinched. He said, in a too loud, overly familiar way, didn't mean to scare you. I spoke my predetermined line, hi Uncle Mike, my bus arrived early.

At his gesture I followed him to a green sedan. Once he'd closed the door, he started in on the rules. He would not tell where we were going. When we got to where we were going I would get out and then walk confidently up the stairs and into the house without knocking. Act like you've been there a hundred times. I nodded. Inside you'll find out what to do next. I'll be waiting when you're done. He then offered up a bandana. He said I would need to get into the backseat and tie it around my head so I couldn't see. Also, I had to lay down flat while he drove.

I was dumbstruck. He pushed the lighter in on the dash and patted his pockets. His face was quite pink. I thought this is not a man suited for any kind of heat. If I didn't follow these instructions to a T, he said, the whole thing was off. He was happy to kick me out right there. He waited. He could tell I was scared. We have to protect ourselves, he said. Give me the money if you're in. My fake uncle stranger started up the car. Like a sheep, I did what I was told without making a peep. Strobes of light came through the blindfold. He sped up and slowed.

I took deep breaths. I began to count the car's turns. I got up to seven before I became confused. Maybe he was turning in circles. I gave up orienting myself and instead called up calming musical images. I hummed to myself songs that I'd liked so much in childhood. Before my closed eyes a montage of balletic actresses in pastel prairie dresses, their skirts spinning away from their bodies like flowers. Dark-haired men gazed fervently. A moment of tragedy in the form of a fresh bouquet laid at a tombstone— Here lies mother. Bless my beautiful hide and then there was that barn dance scene. A June bride is a bride forever.

The breaks squealed as we slowed.

I hopped out and climbed toward the door as if perfectly at ease. There were children playing ball in the otherwise unpopulated street. The air felt heavier than in Old Lyme, sooty. I pulled on the old metal knob and it opened. I was behaving as directed. Behind me I heard the driver pull away.

I found myself in an entryway alone. Before me an interior stairway made of carved wood with a long ribbon of worn carpet connecting the stairs to an upper landing with a row of closed doors, the place made me think of player pianos and high lace collars. I wondered if they were really expecting me. Maybe I'd been conned. My heart was going crazy. Then, I heard a door open and a man's voice call down, did Uncle Mike bring you from the bus station? I responded to my cue and the voice said come on up.

One car led to another ride, one stairway followed the next, and at every turn some man was there, judging me for my mistake of letting a man touch me. I brushed my fingertips against the wall for support. Who knew where I was, what array of implements awaited me. Blades arrayed on an aluminum tray. That morning I'd imagined a doctor's office like the one Marie had taken me to in Grand Junction. Dr. Nilsson had a poster of the human body on his wall and a son one year under me in school. I could be murdered here, quite easily, I realized in a flash. I'd gotten in the car and handed over money, willingly. It wouldn't even be robbery. Complicit in her ruination. I'd be a small story in the paper. Young actress found dead.

The stage manager and Vince would be the only ones to know. I wondered if one of them would tell Karla the truth. Karla would have to identify me at the morgue. She would be the one to call Aunt Marie in Colorado and my father in New Mexico. Tears welled up when I pictured Marie's soft eyes. I was dumb, the dumbest girl in the world. My knees wobbled and I felt faint. My fears always came to me when it was too late to do anything. I kept acting as if this was all normal and I knew what to do. I could feel the presence of the doctor waiting. As soon as I entered he shut the door behind.

It was suffocating in that room where I had the procedure. The windows were closed and the curtains drawn. They were orange and tinted the light that bled through the same color. The room felt like the inside of a pumpkin, hollowed out for a jack-o'-lantern. It smelled of a wet chemical mixed with overcooked food, a meal made down the hall that had drifted here and then stayed put. Liver and onions. A casserole of Campbell's cream soup poured over egg noodles then baked too long. People shouldn't turn on their ovens in the summer, I thought. It poisons the air.

The doctor asked right away if I was ready without preamble or introduction. The doctor. I needed to believe that was what he was, Dr. Nilsson but different. There was nothing medicinal or pristine about the house. My only hope came from the fact he seemed so bored by me. He had a confidence that I hoped came from many years of practice.

He was an old man with tanned skin and a two-tone shirt like what fathers wear when mowing their lawns in advertisements for beer. He must be a retired doctor, I told myself, helping girls out of trouble. He had a thin crumpled-in mouth but, I willed myself to believe, kind eyes. Not that he met my gaze much. It was as if he couldn't stomach it. He coughed thickly and then ordered me to remove my skirt and underwear and lie down on a table that was draped in a yellow rubber sheet. The girl lies down and spreads her legs again and again for different men.

Have you done this before? the doctor asked. I shook my head hard. He patted my knee then left his hand there as he inserted two fingers inside and felt around. Then he began to fiddle with some metal tools on a tray. Relax. Stay quiet and keep your legs apart. Even though the window was closed I could still hear the kids playing in a muffled way. Their oblivious closeness made me feel soiled but also comforted. Maybe if I had to scream they'd tell their mothers.

My neatly folded underwear was tucked inside my purse. The purse was made of straw with fabric trimming sewn around all the edges and a pattern of flowers embroidered on the side. I stroked the flowers with my eyes, only closing them when the sensations became too much. I cried in silence as he scraped away at me. It felt like a razor blade pulled down in small strokes. Like what you do to remove paint from a windowpane. My mother had shown me how to do this once, when she'd plunged us into yet another home beautification project. We put on old clothes and painted the kitchen peach. She showed me how to hold the razor blade carefully between thumb and fingers without getting cut and I felt happy that she trusted me like that. It comes right off when you scrape at an angle, she instructed. It was like that now except my insides were the glass.

Stop moving, the doctor whispered. His voice was terribly firm.

I made myself a movie in my head. It flickered in motion at the same rate as the internal scrapes. I was the star and I was a young girl. She was persecuted by her family for getting pregnant by the man she loved. She who was me was beaten by her father with whatever was handy. He used a coat hanger and then a belt pulled from its loops around the waist. Disgusting whore. It was the way I had glanced, the trick I had of fluttering my lashes. Any man could see I was easy. My movie father beat me because he loved me. I had debased myself. I was a pig who never listened. I turned my blue eyes toward heaven. I'd ruined myself. Trash. This scraping inside was my punishment. At the end of the movie, I died and the audience wept.

I guess I had a good capacity for pain. He didn't give me any more corrections. After the doctor finished, he told me to keep changing my sanitary pads as they'd probably soak through. He said to go to the hospital if I felt really bad after a couple days or if I bled too much. But if they ask, don't tell them anything. Explain it started of its own accord; our lady of immaculate hemorrhaging. What he meant by too much blood I didn't want to know.

I was fine, really. My fake uncle drove me back to the diner where Vince was waiting, sullen and smoking. Neither of us had a thing to say.

In the Delray the radio was turned up loud. I felt nauseous in the twilight. The boat of a car carried us, sliding down the quiet lanes that lead to the bucolic village. The movement was so smooth it was as if a ghost were driving. We rode in a silver coach. Some of the roads had woods beside them, while others had white fences and fields with horses. This landscape was the color of old America, houses of Protestant cream and founding fathers red. The next night the local people in these tidy houses would leave their houses and come up the hill to see us perform *A View from the Bridge*. Vince would kiss me in front of all of them and we'd all know it was pretend.

Blood was accumulating and soaking through the pad. I squeezed my legs together and draped myself onto one side so as little of my bottom touched the seat as possible. I was afraid, even in my pained state, of ruining Vince's white leather interior. I hung out the window and tried not to be sick.

On the radio a new song started. Phil Phillips began to sing about love. The trees turned dark, dark green as the last light of the sun lost itself below the horizon. The East Coast had so many beautiful trees, I thought. This place had so many seasons and so much humidity. The soft air flowed across the grasses that grew up from the marsh edge of the sea.

My father got remarried when I was working in Old Lyme. He called to share the special news. He had met Jeanie Van Fleet in Mesa Arizona. She was a widow, so they matched. She played tennis and hiked and was a real neat woman. She had a son, Matthew, who was a junior in high school and had a knack for science. My father thought I'd get along really well with Jeanie and her boy. My father said I'd meet them soon and all this was a bit of a surprise. He said he knew I was busy with plays and the cost of airline tickets being what they were, I shouldn't worry about visiting. It was going to be a small ceremony after all.

I replied daughter-like, yes of course Dad, that makes sense.

I didn't hate my father, if that's what it seems like. We had our tensions and our estrangement of course. When I was small we didn't talk much because he was busy and I was a child and he had great projects to work on. Then my mother was having a hard time and took me to Marie's. After the suicide what was he supposed to do? Wrap me in his arms and cry and cry and cry? Impossible.

For all those years he gave Aunt Marie and then Karla money to raise me and keep me safe, which they did despite my best efforts. He sent more money straight to me, checks inside Christmas and birthday cards, and I frittered it away on books and clothes and cosmetics.

When I was a child my father's chin was clean-shaven, his blue eyes watery behind thick glasses. They fogged into portholes in the winter. You could barely see him through the reflections, the condensation and the smudges.

Talking to him as his only child felt like that. Like trying to catch his gaze when he'd just come in from the cold. It was hard to tell if he actually wanted to see me. We were polite acquaintances. When confronted with one another, we froze, embarrassed by what the other person knew.

I couldn't be angry so I got sad. He was busy. He was fragile. He had lost my mother as much as I had.

On the phone that day he quizzed me about Connecticut. I said I'd learned a lot about acting. He said, that's terrific. He said we'd better hang up because these long-distance calls cost an arm and a leg.

Congratulations. I hurried the words out. These were the kinds of things normal people said to one another. I am happy for you, Daddy. I will come out for a visit soon. Of course you will, dear, he replied.

I never did though.

———

There are periods when everything happens, especially when you are young. You actually do find the door you were looking for and you walk right through.

How do you enter to be noticed? How do you leave to be remembered after you've gone? What's the best way of fitting your living body into the endless small rectangles controlled by grown men? I began to ask myself such questions in earnest.

Proscenium stages and doorways, arching trees and open windows, a man's arm outstretched as he presses his hand into a wall, all kinds of things can be a frame depending on how you position yourself in relation. If you want people to look you must become your own cinematographer. Allow yourself to be seen in the right light. Position yourself so that spaces pull their colors close around you. Choose to make yourself a beautiful focal point. It's possible, though not easy.

An untethered physical girl finds her calling making scenes. She concocts memorable entries and exits. Crawl, clamor, saunter, arrive. Reveal one's face by turning boldly around with a look over the shoulder. Make those men see you for what you are, or, more effectively, make yourself what they want to see.

There was a moment in Connecticut, after all the convincing, when I found myself alone. I stood looking at myself in the mirror, the blackness of backstage creating a dark universe all around. I told myself, if this is life, if you are already going to spend your time bleeding and crying, at least make it interesting to watch. Make it visible to others. Show yourself. That is the art and the work, to become visible and then withstand the forces of all those penetrating eyes. You have to do it fully or pack it in now.

So, I became a girl who threw open unfamiliar doors and made those on the other side pay attention. And I did it without them knowing I knew. That was the real trick, to appear innocent while working with all my young force.

I walked back and forth across a stage. I wept. I shone. Then, all of a sudden, I was offered a part in a film. A film director had found me in the barn that was a theater. I could not have willed it better.

It happened because Lev saw me for who I was. He was down there in the darkness of the audience, watching alongside all the vacationers in their ginghams and summer sports jackets, and he had seen into me. I was onstage under the blinding lights and enclosed behind the fortified fourth wall. I couldn't have seen him if I'd tried, but he saw me.

It can go the way the stories say, a girl can experience an abrupt change of station. One night she may be clammy with fear in her pink costume, with a ribbon restraining her waterfall of hair, and then the next instant she can be discovered. She flies into the shimmering flow of a man's vision and it pulls her out forever, far beyond what she'd ever imagined. She never returns to the shore she started from.

———

It was unglamorously glamorous though, at first. I went to a dingy room on Forty-First Street. A conspiracy of men sat around drinking coffees out of paper cups, laughing and whispering. They were dressed carelessly in nice clothes. Slacks-clad legs crossed and worn leather shoes sticking out from beneath the folding table. Before them were sheets of paper with notes and doodles. I felt like I'd wandered into an all-boys school.

Thanks for coming in, sweetheart, I raved about you when I got back from Old Lyme. I asked if they'd like me to read something. The director said no, forget your acting training and talk to me naturally, so I did. We talked for half an hour. I made him laugh.

That evening the phone rang and it was him. He said I got the part.

Over the years I learned that this was something Lev loved to do, deliver the news personally. It excited him to hear raw elation flow through the spiral of the telephone cord. He loved to be the magnanimous daddy bestowing blessings, changing fortunes with a word. He chose. Others were chosen.

You're terrific, he told me, just terrific. We will shoot in the spring, he said, in France. Ever been? You're teasing me Mr. Samaras, I gushed. Call me Lev, he said, because we are going to work together and I can't stand formalities.

Years later, Lev and I got married. We are married still even though I am sleeping with this cowboy in this western movie and he's been with God knows how many other women.

My heart goes still sometimes when I remember all this. I cannot feel it beat even though I know it must be working. I was so happy.

Lev was born Lev Dimitrios Samaras in October in the village of Tsagkarada, on the slope of the Pelion mountains in northeastern Greece. His father's family was from the city of Thessaloniki, where his people had lived for all time. They would have lived there still if not for war. Out of desperation, anxiety, and sheer terror, Lev's parents bundled the family up and fled from Turkish soldiers. They did not go south to Athens but rather quit the whole region, going first to England, and then on to America.

Of England Lev remembered heavily curtained rooms where his parents plotted. His mother massaged her husband's shoulders. She took down letters as he dictated. His father had business interests with a British Greek man, but it was going badly. Amid all the calamity it was as if his parents had forgotten they had children. Lev's older sisters shoved him out the door, forcing him to take long cold walks so his parents could think.

Lev described to me these distinct sense memories, his sweater spangled with droplets, his oldest sister molding his hand around pencils, showing him the shapes of letters and then words, guiding his hand across the page into some kind of penmanship.

He recalled some of the boys on the street, hands around his throat in a playful, painful way that felt erotic. The small of a back exposed in wrestling. They stayed in England a number of years in a kind of limbo until his father's ship came in, entrepreneurially speaking. His parents moved the family to be close to more family on Long Island.

Lev threw himself into the project of belonging. His father too embraced his adopted country's pastimes and mores, at least the ones that suited him. His mother and sisters drew closer to one another. They abandoned the men in favor of a feminine secrecy they could maintain against this crass new continent. Because of an Americanized uncle, Lev's father rooted for the Yankees and at first Lev went along, but eventually he changed his allegiances to the Dodgers because he didn't feel like celebrating such obvious winners.

Lev's father died of a heart attack halfway through Lev's first year in college.

My trip to Amsterdam was my first time in the air. I felt abstract, more electrical than human. I had taken some Dexedrine before boarding. Cup of coffee in the airport and in the air. I pictured myself as a particle speeding along. I remember my father trying to teach me bits of science. He would pose physics questions, there was one about twins, one who stays on earth and the one who flies into space. The question had to do with which one would age faster. There was another question about a person in a vehicle, walking in the opposite direction from the way they were headed. If a girl walks fifteen feet down the aisle, heading to a lavatory at the back of the plane to powder her nose, and she's walking at the rate of three miles an hour, while the plane hurtles forward toward Europe traveling at a rate of six hundred miles per hour, how fast is she traveling toward her destiny? How much older will she be than her phantom twin when they reunite back on earth?

Out of the crowds at the airport emerged a red-faced man holding up a paper sign with my name written on it in firm block letters. He was the driver tasked with taking me from the city to our filming location, a village a few hours away.

I remember him alternately cursing the traffic in Dutch and quizzing me about the United States in strongly accented English. He queried if I liked the president and I said of course. He represents the youth of the country better than anyone ever has. And his wife is perfection. He hummed some air through his teeth and said all this tension with Russia was no good for Europe.

He had friends who were Polish, he said, and I didn't understand what he meant so just nodded. He offered me a cigarette as he lit a new one off the butt he was finishing. A young man on a motorcycle barely avoided being hit by a truck right in front of us and the driver expelled a fresh burst of expletives. These young people, he said, act as if death isn't real.

When, finally, he deposited me at the country inn where I had a room waiting, I passed out on the quilt-covered bed without even taking off my shoes.

I slept as if dead until the housekeeper's knock jolted me awake. I was on the continent of my ancestors, of bloodshed and my favorite movies. My work was about to begin. I was white as the sheets tangled around me.

Saint Barbara was shot in the outskirts of the city of 's-Hertogenbosch over one spring and early summer. We did most of the scenes in and around a leaky old brick factory that had lain disused since the war. We stayed at the inn and had proper meals and a gentle way of life during production.

In preparation for *Saint Barbara*, Lev organized the cast and select crew around a folding table. There, for hours each day, we talked. Or rather, Lev and the other actors talked and I listened and read and worked to stay afloat in the depths of these intellectual conversations. I drank coffee, made notes, and spoke when spoken to. I sat beside Lev because he told me to.

Lev talked about alienation from the body, the kind that could make great violence possible. He described French women, tarred and feathered; their heads shaved because they'd slept with German soldiers. He and the man who played my father argued about industry as a new religion. Spirit or *gheist* was something else, it had moved through the ages attaching to this practice or the other.

Lev had us read aloud, sections of *The Human Condition*, poems by Brecht, Rilke, and Christine de Pizan. He gave me a book of short stories by Robert Musil to read at night. All the stories were about lust and death, vacation towns and the overheated intricacies of women's inner lives. We analyzed images in the Grimms' version of "Rapunzel": long golden hair that forms a rope; eyes pierced by thorns; the voice of an unseen singer emerging from a tower. Lev spoke with great feeling about what the film was about to him. The script was spare but we read and workshopped what was on the page in order to capture the mood he wanted.

Mist hung over spongy fields. The ground emanated moisture under the pale sun. Clouds billowed above like smoke that wanted to retreat back into the chimney. Weak-boned trees hung around the factory entry waiting to be cut down and burned.

Inside the long low building there were shelves upon shelves that were built for drying bricks. The tunnels these shelves lined went on and on, aimed toward a black void termination. A person could walk away from the camera and grow smaller until they disappeared into the darkness. It looked like an art book's example of a vanishing point, perspective and all that. When we yelled it echoed.

Lev said once that he saw making art as something like mining, hard labor, the stripping-away of layers that conceal what is precious. We want only the gems.

It was a week or two into shooting when Lev seduced me. He asked me to stay after one of our cast meetings, one thing led to another, and he fucked me quite romantically against a back wall behind a curtain.

Lev loved everyone and I was someone so it was natural.

Lev had what people call bedroom eyes. Celadon green and fringed with thick lashes. They seemed to let others in, to absorb what they saw, to well up with feeling. Windows to the soul, people said. Sure. Sensitivity was assumed because of his features, which had nothing to do with his deeper personality and had so much more to do with the beautiful eyes he'd inherited from his mother's side of the family.

Like everyone, I loved to feel Lev's eyes on me, when they were behind the camera's viewfinder or in the semidarkness of his room. It was intoxicating to feel his look.

Others on the set knew what was happening, the director sleeping with his actress, but it was fine. It wasn't serious, or rather, the filming was while the sex wasn't. To him at least. I made sure to appear light, careless.

Lev was in the war when he was young and that was how he'd become a director. He had joined the army because all his friends were doing it and because his father had died of a heart attack. Because he spoke Greek and some Italian, and English of course, and because he had learned in college how to handle a camera and develop film too, he was assigned the role of camera operator in the Signal Corp. The army sent him back to Europe where he'd come from.

The army moved Lev around the old world. He traveled with cameras, and leather cases holding rolls of film and other technological supplies slung around his person. He was charming and quick. He came to love important feelings and high-intensity work. He followed powerful men, skirted bomb craters, he slept in muddy fields sometimes and other times in fancy buildings that had been broken open and wrecked by this or that army. He saw many kinds of horrors through various military lenses. He came to know the smells of different kinds of death, burnt or bloated, poisoned or starved.

In the last month of the war, while traveling with an infantry division, Lev Samaras came to enter a camp called Ohrdruf. The army's trucks rolled along slow. Lev was riding in the back of the truck, facing backward, seeing only what was behind him.

He couldn't see the gates until he'd passed through but he could sense they were passing into a netherworld because of the smell. It came in waves; it entered his body as the winds shifted.

Chemicals and burnt railroad ties, petrol and gangrenous flesh, quicklime and feces and the smell of a deep, all-encompassing rot. Filth and sewage had mixed with the mud. The trucks rolling in kicked up a fine dust. Bodies were heaped. Lev saw that right away, though it took a minute for his understanding to catch up. Amid the piles some people were alive, and they waved to him. Quivering, stick-like hands emerged out from heaps of the dead. Living corpses walked on their spindles toward them with their arms outstretched.

Lev's friend McMurtry leaned over and whispered from behind a handkerchief he had held against his mouth. Don't touch anyone. They have cholera. The drivers were afraid that there was typhus in the dust. There was disease there, they were not wrong. If a person was that sick and thin, McMurtry said, they couldn't keep the food down. If they eat what we have it'll kill them. Don't touch. Record everything you see, he whispered. McMurtry's hands trembled violently. Lev's felt turned to stone.

The spring day was vivid and smooth as if filmed through a gas blue filter. Lev worked automatically. He used all the film he had on him, retrieving more from his stockpile in the truck whenever a roll ran out.

German guards the Americans had turned into prisoners were gathered around a pit. Down in the hole were burned things, papers and tools and human beings, all jumbled together and still smoldering. The German men were a mix of too young and too old, misshapen and angular. When Lev pointed the camera at them they did not turn away. They looked beyond him toward the woods on the other side of the fence. A mound of corpses towered beside them. The ground near the pit was wet, wherever Lev stepped was a slippery mush.

He spent hours looking through his viewfinder. What he saw he could not have borne with the naked eye. Some of his friends did, but it hurt them. What McMurtry saw during the war damaged him within. Later in life he turned to drink and silence. His children were scared of him. The damage was done in a flash but the effects rippled out and out over decades and continents. It could not be borne to see what was done, and yet it was done and it was seen.

What Lev saw he absorbed too. He took in with his pores, his liver and spleen, through his lungs. He absorbed the blood on the walls into his own blood. Only the camera protected him, the little machine stood between him and the full force of that reality. Lev felt himself vaporized. He became a cloud of steam.

After the camp he was sent to the town where the German officers had lived. There he absorbed the red curtains in their living rooms and their pictures in frames of happy friendly everyday life. The Americans arrested the mayor. The man claimed to know nothing despite all the poisonous smoke. He was innocent, he said, only the mayor of an insignificant hamlet. He had no power. There were so many people Lev had to film who said they knew nothing. The mayor had a glassy stare.

The night of his arrest the mayor committed suicide in his jail cell, hung himself with a belt looped around the window bars. His neck turned purple and stretched long. The next morning Lev photographed that too.

In those last months of the war, I felt calm, smoother than I had at any time in my life, Lev said. It was as if an ice pick had been hammered through my eye socket. It was as if the hands that reached toward me had ice-pick fingers. They slipped into my brain and lobotomized me.

Though my brain stopped working my body appeared fine. I slept each night like an animal in a den, woke wide at the call, did fifty push-ups and the same number of sit-ups in the gray dawn. I dressed with deliberation, buttoned myself all the way up. Tucked in my layers so that as little skin as possible showed. I was so tidy. My body lay beneath my undershirt, my shirt and jacket. My thighs, which were healthy muscle covered with smooth flesh, moved decisively beneath my underwear and pants. My feet were safe within thick socks and sturdy boots. At the table I cleaned my plate without a wasted bite. I ate but did not taste. When we had it, I drank but did not get drunk. I laughed at the jokes told by other men. I kept everything I possessed in tip-top condition. I cleaned my camera with a tiny brush, Lev said. I was commended.

Lev wrote a letter to his mother where he described it all, as well as he was able. His hands shook. His mother read the letter to neighbors. These stories were not in the news then. His mother understood, she believed. Her American neighbors knew it was bad but somehow they doubted too, she could sense their disbelief. Though they lived side-by-side for another twenty years, until Mr. and Mrs. Kostas retired to Florida, Lev's mother never really trusted them after that.

After Lev returned from the war, he knew the only thing he wanted was to make movies. He was all too aware that for film he needed money, but also social connections. Lev's ambitions have a violence in them, but like I said, he's a consummate seducer and has those eyes that can pull almost anyone in.

Lev got married. That was the first thing. He found for a bride a well-heeled daughter of the upper Midwest who was living in New York after graduating college. Mary Grace Mixon was no great beauty but she was full of lust and had the security of a sporting goods fortune behind her. She had also the attractive wish to frustrate her family's executive ambitions. Lev noted that right away. Her parents wanted her to marry a nice stockbroker. Instead, she married a silver-tongued immigrant with haunted insomnia.

Lev was a real artist, Grace sighed. She loved him as a war hero. She could practically orgasm just looking at him. She'd attended Vassar, she'd heard Camus speak. She'd read. God knows the stories Lev spun her. God knows the pillow talk.

Despite any doubts his in-laws may have had about him, Mary Grace was the only child of Mr. and Mrs. Mixon, so they were not prepared to treat their daughter's veteran husband too hard.

Mary Grace shielded Lev from anything mundane. Her easy habits and friendly account in the vaulted Central Savings Bank gave Lev a great sense of possibility. He made his way into the film world. He made friends and found acolytes. He bought rounds and stayed up all night. Cabaret shows and jazz, discreet brothels with male friends and art shows with his wife on his arm, apartment parties in the village and trips to the track for a laugh. Whatever was on offer was interesting to him. He charmed people because he seemed not to need anything from them. A cool, gas-blue light burned inside him.

He auditioned for roles in movies with an electric carelessness that caught directors' attention. He could be insane one moment then fall into joking. He got parts but they did not hint at the full career that would follow. In his first appearance on-screen, he plays the ne'er-do-well husband of a woman losing her mind. Next, he was cast in a noir as a sweet younger brother whose death motivates the real star to go on a journey of revenge.

Lev's swagger was always at play in his screen persona. He wore a disguise and a smirk that came across as authentic. A motif emerged across pictures of him undressing. Directors like to show him halfway, pulling on or off clothes. In one scene he's shown donning the suit of a man who's committed suicide in the other room not moments before. Lev was a cuckoo, breaching the confines of the once-safe nest and taking what he needed. At home Grace dolled herself up in lace peignoirs she bought from Henri Bendel. After fucking her silly Lev would go to his office and scribble away all night.

With his friend Peter on the phone, they'd plot ways to make the movies they wanted to see. Theirs would be superior to Hollywood's big productions. They would make deadly precise, devastating films about the secret fascism of America. Their characters would lose their minds, and in their madness expose the rot of this puritanical, paranoid, oppressive freedom they were all enjoying. His characters would be men and women trying to crawl out of the bomb craters. Only very occasionally would they succeed.

During *Saint Barbara* I had fantasies about being Lev's perfect mistress, not only on the film set but back in New York too. When I breathed the possibility Lev laughed. He dismissed me as a kid. He already had two of those along with a wife in the city. There's no room. He and Mary Grace had a school-age boy and a girl. You're making an old man happy now, he said. When I said I thought I had an old soul he patted my head.

You need to find a young husband, Lev said. In the meantime, he said, us screwing was good for my acting. It was. Wasn't it? He made me cum in the dressing room, silently, hard before scenes so that I looked unkempt, loose, touched by a spiritual intensity on camera.

I should have felt guilty but didn't. Mary Grace was a grown woman, he an adult man who'd been to war. Married feelings were theirs to manage. We were playing. He acquired for me the pill. Relax baby, he whispered. There's a new way of life that's open to you now. Good, like that. Look up. Feel where the light hits you and relax your mouth. Other men will appreciate what I'm teaching you.

I loved him I suppose because he was the director, meaning teacher, daddy, and judge. He described power and wielded it so I could see. Honey, this is what movies are, don't forget that. Power, magic, a capturing of reality itself. He built his movie like a court case. He put us on trial. When I was barely anything, he gave me the role of a saint and made me his temporary mistress, so I loved him. On rainy evenings we linked arms. He held up an umbrella over me. How could I resist? Everybody had to get protection somehow.

He made scenes. Yelled and then laughed at my reactions. I'd see what we experienced repeated years later in films by actors he cast. I could picture him easily with other women and men, collaborators, buddies who wrangled with art. I could see the ways he seduced them all.

Lev never seemed to sleep. He had multiple newspapers stacked up each morning beside his breakfast tray. He made us tiny coffees with a silver espresso maker he balanced on a hot plate because he declared the inn's stuff undrinkable.

I was playing a woman who has visions and conviction. She was an ordinary girl but was also a saint. She was the first Rapunzel locked in a tower.

Lev took the religious story of Saint Barbara and twisted it into strange and haunting film. In Lev's version, the tower becomes a country house with many chimneys. He talked to me about male domination and mysticism, Greeks and barbarians. The film was set in modern times but had echoes and references to the ancient all over it: there were cannons and chalices; thornbushes, staffs, roses, and evil eyes; windmills and ships with sails; crosses and carvings in caves. There were dream scenes and everyday scenes and the film editing intercut the two. When watching you didn't always know when was now and when was then.

Barbara the character was a daughter with no mother and a jealous father. Her father was an industrialist who had collaborated with fascists during the war. He had gotten away with it. Though he had much power he was preoccupied with controlling his daughter. He wanted to stop her from reading and thinking and giving money to the poor. He decided to hide her away. For her own good, he said.

Her father arranged that she be given food and drink but kept inside their mansion.

Though Barbara lived in isolation she did not waste the time she had. She meditated. Through her window she took in the world, absorbing the quotidian practices of the villagers, the cycles of days and nights, months and seasons, and above it all the movement of the stars and planets in the blue heavens.

One day she was struck by a beam of divine knowledge, the light of God.

Her father knows nothing of his child's inner life but he suspects she had secret depths. That was what he was determined to tame. He believes a daughter must do a father's bidding. In his daily life he dines with generals and judges. He is a captain of industry and feels he must make moral sacrifices to further the objectives of the nation. He believes he can marry her off to someone who will get her pregnant and that will tame her intensity. He conspires to marry her to an appropriate man. Her father brings her suitors, powerful men who sit in rooms he frequents, who represent good families. She rejects them. She begs her father to release her. He relents somewhat, says she can go out and learn about life. He thinks that with this show of trust she will learn to appreciate his wisdom.

One night Barbara comes home drunk with her long hair cut short like a gamine. She announces to her father she's given her jewelry to some young revolutionaries. She'd had an awakening.

All his patience and generous feelings are gone. He begins to beat her. It is terrible.

Barbara twists out of her father's grasp and runs. She takes shelter in a cave. In Lev's version the cave of the original is transposed into a concrete bunker deep beneath his factory.

Her father and his friends, the police chief and military men, gather at the entry. They want to punish this bad woman but are afraid to pursue her. A night passes and then a day. Inside, sore and parched, desperate yet filled with visions, Barbara cries out. A voice answers from another world.

At the end of the saint's story the father murders the daughter. But then he in turn is struck down by God. In the film I cut my hair and my father slits my throat. He then dies himself. His factory burns down with him inside. In the saint's legend he is struck by a bolt of lightning out of the clear blue sky.

——

Because of her faith and martyrdom and the electric death of her father by God's hand, Barbara is the patron saint of miners and bomb makers, soldiers with guns, and anyone who faces death through work. Barbara is invoked for protection from cave-ins and shocks and explosions. She is depicted on holy cards with canons and palm fronds and a tower with three windows for the Father, Son, and Holy Spirit.

When Lev talked to us it was clear he'd been churning these images around in his mind for a long time. I didn't always follow but I trusted the atmosphere he created. Barbara's name, he explained, also inspired the name barbiturate, the sleeping pill. The German scientist Adolf von Baeyer, Lev told me, visited a tavern on Saint Barbara's feast day after first synthesizing the drug. Either that, or he met a pretty barmaid named Barbara and named it after her.

I meditated on how I might integrate these layers of information into my own self and somehow press it all into my performance in the film.

I think I acted well because Lev recognized my lack of innocence, the black hole at the center of me that was made by my mother. Rather than being repelled by it Lev was drawn in. He had a hole too. Many people, he said, had these wounds in their being. You could see the signs if you knew what to look for, he said. It was what we laughed at, or how we shuddered when surprised. We who bore the mark betrayed ourselves subtly, emitted a different scent. He could smell the grief all over me and it made him want to tear me open. To look into the wound with his camera. I wanted him to. It was transcendent to be seen.

Lev said northern Europe was full of human voids, the living dead, and it was understood by the inhabitants. Only the Americans thought life on earth could go back to normal.

The northern world had veins of silver. Cold white skin, blue and pink undertones that mark those not meant for the sun. These people carry their histories draped around them like heavy dense shawls. They had in their souls prayer books and peat fires, eggs for market and eggs for home, noxious gasses, and hard beatings. They had memories of unwanted babies flung by their heels into the darkest part of the woods. Everyone knew. After the war nothing could be denied.

The father shimmers between strength and weakness, Lev said, senility and guile. They are men who see their end coming, who know their children need help in growing, but instead cling to power and use all their will to oppress and control. When the child sees something new, a radiant truth, the jealous father cannot forgive because he suffers and is too jaded to hope. He would as soon kill his daughter as look at her. So where are we now with the old myths, the old gods?

Fathers are at their most awful when rising from their deepest decay. He rushes into the yard dressed only in half-pulled-up pants and a sweat-damp nightshirt, threatening to kill all the young men. He threatens to kill his daughter because her radiant sexuality shines on the future. His shirt conceals sinewed arms. Though aged, the father is still six feet tall and barrel-chested. His grip is like a vice. Even far from the height of his power, he is terrifying. It doesn't matter what you think, Lev said.

For all Lev's wildness he kept the set disciplined, clean. We all agreed that we could be uncontrolled in our art, but beneath it remained a core of work and trust. I never even smoked while working except on the day we shot the last scene before my death. The scene had to encapsulate a willingness to die resisting tyranny. It had to bear the weight of all of Lev's vision. I was so petrified I developed a stutter.

We did three takes and I only got worse with each. Eventually Lev sent the crew away for a break. He had me drink two huge gulps of vodka. He held my shoulders and whispered, imagine your mother is here with you, bring that emotion to the surface baby, let me see. The task of the actress is to bring real emotion to imaginary circumstances. He brought back the people who were necessary. We breathed in the dark until everything was set and then I wailed. I lost myself completely.

In the dark of the cave, sore and parched, Barbara cried out for God.

I cannot remember what I did but Lev was satisfied and just like that, I was no longer needed. I was finished on set. The crew clapped for me and I got embraced all around but could not stop crying and had to retreat to my hotel room.

On our last night together, Lev worked urgently over my naked body. I did the same to him, matching and perhaps surpassing his lust. I was so grateful and terrified. Bruised and triumphant. I was as crass as I'd always been afraid I really was, deep down.

I fucked him like it was my only way to stay alive, as if I was on my way to the gallows at dawn. I floated. I kissed. I was fresh and open, dewy and desperate to make this sensation last. I was a modern slut channeling an ancient saint.

The sheets were all wet when we ended. I went to the window to open the curtains. It was midsummer and the sun rising started to make the fields outside glow a blurred honey yellow. It was five forty-five in the morning.

After *Saint Barbara* I got another job right away. I was cast in a small French production that aimed to be hip and modern and perhaps get some attention in the States. Some of the actors' voices were overdubbed with English voices because their accents were strong. I played a girlfriend who had nothing much to do but pout and be American. There was a whole gaggle of women.

From other actresses I learned many things about the current style. They showed me how to wing my eyelids with black liner. One's lips were meant to stay uncolored or the softest pink. I bought dark tights and tall leather boots. They told me where to shop for underthings. They were sweet but the issue of language sat on my lap like a heavy bag I could not squirm free of.

I was hired for just a few weeks but it gave me an excuse to stay in Paris. If there was one such picture maybe there would be another. I told myself I was learning the language but mostly I was writing in a journal and drinking so many coffees. It seemed like the thing to do, waving for a waiter and having them bring another brown cup glazed white inside like a seashell. I positively vibrated with the effects of caffeine. I was twenty-three years old and it was September.

At a party one evening, I was introduced to Simon Tremblay. One of the girls from the film said this is my friend from school, he writes and he's terribly depressed. Maybe you can cheer him up. Simon's father was English and so I could talk to him, and talk I did.

We were out on a narrow balcony. I remember orbs of lemon-yellow light polka-dotting the black night. It was warm and late. Simon didn't seem depressed; he was leaning with both elbows on the metal railing and making quiet jokes.

There was a commotion inside. We hustled back in and found that Simon's friend Thomas had gotten his nose broken in a bout of soccer horseplay. Thomas and a little crowd of men had been in the apartment's kitchen pantomiming their past heroics on the pitch. There was a collision of elbow and face followed by a burst of blood.

Someone turned the record player off, and the mood went sober and quiet except for Thomas and the nose breaker, both of whom were cackling like crows.

The hosts were consulting on which hospital one might reasonably go to at this late hour. Ice from a bucket had been wrapped in a towel. A girl was on the telephone seeking official guidance. Thomas was laughing still but his face was deathly white. Simon tried to get him to sit still and hold his head back but he kept moving around, standing to get his cigarettes from a pocket and then again for a lighter. When helpers tried to get Thomas to hold the ice to his nose he swore and pushed them away. The whole front of his nice blue sports shirt was soaked through. On the wall was a well-defined handprint. From his head had come blood. It had pooled, ruby red and perfectly oval on the black and white tiles. Like a crime scene. Those not directly involved gathered on the room's edges, gawking but afraid to step in, lest they contaminate the evidence. We mustn't panic, Simon said, it looks much worse than it is.

Decisions were made. As everyone shuffled out, giving thanks to the host with cheek kisses and apologies for the sober ending, Simon grabbed my elbow. He and a few others had taken the task of shepherding Thomas to the hospital. Their disordered ward should get an X-ray, or at the very least a bottle of pain pills. Would I like to go? It was not such a romantic first date. Simon shrugged. But he wanted to spend more time with me. I recalled that book from childhood, Madeline being rushed to the hospital in the middle of the night for a burst appendix. Miss Clavel and Dr. Cohn. Vines and lines and girls in Paris. I had nowhere else to be on this entire continent and felt so awake. Simon was handsome and Thomas would be fine in the end. Why not go? I did.

Just as Lev had advised, here was a young man, a husband dropped before me in a scene of injury and action.

Simon proposed after only a few months, and we got married at city hall in December. I wore a fur coat and a mini dress. His suit was navy and slim. Thomas the broken-nosed boy, now healed, took our picture. Simon's mother Fabienne and his cousin Apoline took us out to lunch afterward. When I called Karla to tell her the news I said I was overjoyed. I don't know if she believed me.

What I fell in love with, and could not distinguish from Simon himself, was a sense of ritual and habit, the assurance that someone knew how things were done. With Simon there were answers. He had them and so did France.

Church Bells rang at 7:00 A.M. and 7:00 P.M. each day and that was called the Angelus. They chimed too at all sorts of other times but there was always a reason, whether I could divine it or not. Men swept the sidewalks with tall brooms made of sticks. If a destination was less than half an hour away we walked, and if it was more we took the Métro. Simon found cabs excessive. Say hello to the shopkeeper when you enter a store. Say goodbye. If it was raining, Simon's mother told me gently, I must tie a silk scarf over my hair in addition to carrying an umbrella or else I would get frizz. Dinner was always at eight fifteen in the evening and we must never be late, especially when his mother invited us over.

I did what I was told. Simon thought if my French got better I could get roles in movies here. Critics had liked *Saint Barbara*, but for all we'd put into it, the film had come and gone too quickly. It was a strange style and the film people I met were all mad for Hollywood. Lev was a strange one. I tried to explain the art I thought he was making.

I labored with my speech and understanding. Some days I could understand the feelings but not respond, others I could babble on without taking in. I struggled to assemble the simplest feelings into words. Simon spoke English with me to a point, but when he and his friends got tired of humoring me and took off, galloping away in fast, slang-filled French night after night in the café they liked best around the corner from our apartment, I would slip into a luxurious muteness. I was beside him but alone. I thought much more than I spoke and Simon found that alluring until he didn't.

Simon's mother Fabienne had Cupid's-bow lips she still painted as if it were the silent era. She'd been beautiful before the war and was still, though in the stricken, haunted way that was so common of mothers. Thomas's father was an American, from Baltimore originally, who'd died of TB after the war, as had Thomas's older brother.

Her apartment was a kind of memorial. At first glance it looked chic but the more time I spent there the more I realized it was all fixed in time. She refused to refresh anything, to let go of what had fallen apart. All she did was rearrange the elements she'd inherited. The glass in some pictures had hairline breaks. The bottoms of the cream brocade curtains were water stained from long-ago leaks. Horsehair poked from the fraying edges of the arm chairs. Porcelain lamps that didn't work but were just for show stood on brittle carved side tables. I found it all disturbing, but Simon wouldn't hear a whisper of criticism.

We should go to the café, Fabienne said on some Saturday afternoon. But in the next breath she sighed, no. Café Mercier is all sticky and crass. And the clientele at Pleyel is wretched now, better to stay in. Whatever you'd like, Simon said, and she'd disappear into the kitchen to prepare a pot of yellow-colored tisane and biscuits, bringing them back to the sitting room arranged on a delicate patterned plate.

I had brought a box of pastries tied with a string as a gift. Simon had assured me they were her favorite, but she got upset and said her headache was terrible and she couldn't take anything too rich. She said she might give them to the neighbor. Then she and Simon stopped speaking slow enough for me to follow along. I cannot blame them for that.

I think Simon married me partly to antagonize his mother. She too had married a foreigner and his father had all but ruined her life. I was a girl she found unsuitable. Not in a way that she was even angry with me about. It was him she chided, for making the mistake of me. Thomas retreated into a netherworld whenever he was confronted with his mother. It was just the two of them and their secret codes. Her speech spun around what she wanted to but could never do. A tight, depressive loop of suggestion and negation. Still, he loved her, much more than he did me, it went without saying.

People died that year. I kept noting them down in my journal until I stopped, not because I wasn't paying attention but because I feared that writing all these deaths encouraged more. Sylvia Plath in Primrose Hill and Patsy Cline in a plane crash, just thirty at the time. The old pope died of stomach cancer but then was replaced by another, just the same, bald and broad at the ears, dressed officially in white and red.

Over that summer people kept dying in United States violence and I could only look on through the rolled-up telescope we call the newspaper. My home planet of a country was burning, everyone could see, but from this distance the heat just looked like light. Someone shot Medgar Evers. Guard units on alert, headlines began, as disorder follows the mourning march of slain civil rights leader. Clubs and dogs used on marchers. Simon and I left the city for the month of August and then someone bombed little girls in church. I put the paper down and went out for a walk, my nerves shaking like the leaves about to fall.

Edith Piaf died. The day after the news you could hear her voice emanating from every record player in Paris. The crowds outside the cemetery the day she was buried made it feel like a national holiday. The aftermath of flowers was monumental.

It felt so green and damp in the city, lush decay with rain and moss growing on stone graves. Paris kept their dead so close at hand. The cemeteries were places you could just go and visit, walk through when you tired of looking at the living. I never got tired of these miniature neighborhoods filled with crypt houses done up in different styles with pretty stained glass and romantic sculptures.

In November Karla died of a stroke. Her friend, Margot's mother, was the one who telephoned me with the news. The next evening,

I spent all day in bed with the curtains drawn. I dithered about flying back. It was so expensive on the one hand, but she had taken care of me on the other. In an unfocused way, I worried that if I left France I'd never return. Simon had been frustrated with me. He was not openly argumentative, just delicately disdainful, and that was worse. I wished for fights because from them could come apologies and make-up kisses.

As I was drifting the telephone rang. It was Simon on the other end, telling me in a great rush that something had happened and I needed to come so we could see what was happening. He was afraid to say more. I threw on a haphazard outfit.

Simon and I didn't own a TV, he said it ruined the style of the home, so we watched the coverage at a café around the corner. I remember how all the tiny black-and-white figures seemed trapped in the square of the set. Cramped, unsure camera angles with too many people coming and going from the frame. Cars and static, men in suits and static. The reporters struggled to name everyone, to narrate the situation. They seemed harried, sweaty, they read quotes. Each piece of news traveled through a series of human filters, a mess of stumbling shock, fragments, and translation. Assassins' bullets, they said. Kennedy, the president of the United States, his limp body in his wife's arms. The open car in the middle of a road. He had been taken to Parkland Hospital, the reporter said. I smoked so many cigarettes that eventually I had to run to the café toilet and vomit. Now everyone knows some version of the story, even if explanations and conspiracies still compete for our belief. But over those first days you could see the struggle to make the story coherent playing out among the people most practiced in control. Senators lurched. Men in trim suits mumbled. Newscasters' jaws hung loose.

We must have gone home to sleep, but I don't recall. I just remember the TV. The hours and days between the first shock and the funeral passed without understanding more despite the growing mountain of news. Then it was morning in Washington and afternoon in Paris the day they buried him. The military drums were muffled; the bagpipes faint. Jets shrieked overhead. The flag-draped casket looked like it was made of lead. It looked like it weighed so much more than it logically should. The soldiers carrying it tread slowly, afraid and swaying in unison. Jackie you couldn't see at all between her black veil and the TV's static.

Simon and I got a divorce. We agreed we could not go on. After that we never saw one another again. I struggle now to remember his face, or what had so moved me about him.

I flew back to New York and took a cab to Suzanna's. There was no other place for me. It was January 7th and dry Christmas trees lay piled on the frozen curb, waiting for the garbagemen to heave their needle-shedding bodies into the truck.

Suzanna had gone to work but she'd left a key under the mat and made a bed for me on her couch in the room she used as an art studio. Light streamed through a stained-glass panel hung in front of the east-facing window. It made the wall glow green and pink in the mornings. I huddled under the striped blanket and watched the steam from my teacup swirl upward. It was as if I was back in the time of Mira, as if nothing had changed except me. I was so much older. I couldn't even cry.

Over the years I'd constructed and abandoned so many routines. Some have been healthful and others destructive, though I don't always know which was which. There was the time of ballet and the Hollywood diet, Jack LaLanne and brute starvation, vodka spritzers and calisthenics, bean sprouts and Benzedrine. I've dabbled in grapefruit diets, measured-out portions of cruciferous vegetables, sugar cubes dripped with LSD, psychotherapy and walking everywhere, never taking subways. Every experiment exacts its price. Substances give and take and your body is left with the residue.

I was not raised with defined rituals. In childhood I had only a sprinkle of my mother's lapsed Catholicism, the faint mist of it on my cheeks. On the other side I had the hard beam of my father's science. He didn't believe in God. Matter was a whir of particles he said. Physics would explain reality while human beings fussed around with their fairy stories. Between them I had no real model of practice.

Each day during this Western shoot I start with some yoga. When the sun comes through the window I rouse myself even though I am exhausted. I put on long johns and a sweater when I creep out of bed. Cold moves up from floorboards into my bare feet.

I have liked yoga since the first time I tried it. Its real power is in repetition. You have to do it over and over to feel even a little. You keep practicing and things change, bit by bit. The body becomes more flexible and gentle, as does, hopefully, the mind. Though, as my teacher says, there is no separation.

I start with sun salutations. I can smell, when my skin gets warm, the aftereffects of Jake. Confident sweat, he makes me feel tender. I feel tender toward him because I know what we have is going to end.

My palms press into the ground. I step back and get distracted by the grit on the floor. Jake, the way he is, makes me want to tell the whole story up to the present. Just because a task is impossible doesn't mean I don't want to try. And I think he will understand not just the glamorous parts but the periods of inertia, the dead ends and delusions.

I want to share with Jake all the sensual moments stored in me.

Life went faster after my return. Experience came to resemble endurance cinema, maybe a work of Jacques Rivette or one of Miklós Jancsó films in which the camera keeps moving along with the actors in a series of tracking shots. A reel of film runs from the beginning to the end and everything happens in one go.

One reel ends and another begins. After a certain number of reels, the film ends.

I like these directors because they worked with peaks and valleys of attention. You could go to sleep in the theater and wake up and the film was still going on, still unspooling in the dark. A stream flows from the heights to the valley. Men enter and depart the frame on horseback as women in festive garb snake around green hillocks doing a ritual dance. A character speaks of danger, a time he almost died. As a soldier he fought through icy water, almost drowning and seeing others around him get pulled beneath. He smelled burnt flesh. A flock of birds rises from a tree behind him. The wild grasses shake as he speaks. He speaks of a long-ago war, but the audience knows that one war reverberates with others. In the distance a military helicopter lands.

As an actor I imagine working in this way gives a kind of release. The director isn't asking for something perfect, rather they ask you to be alive to the moment for a certain period. You have no time for fear. You have to just keep going. There is no more acting, only motion through time, only being present.

In that period, I got extra thin by living on caffeine and fruit, melba toast, and vodka spritzes. When I went with Suzanna to parties people said I looked terrific and all that French style suited me. I auditioned for some movies and plays. I found work. I dressed up, I held objects at trade shows, I appeared fleetingly on

a TV show where I wore a bikini and got hit in the face with a pie.
I got some parts in films. They were of dubious quality, but at least
I was working. I kept acting without fulfilling my early promise. I
don't care to remember too much about *The Monte Carlo Proposal, Sunday Morning,* or *The Witchcraft of Salem Village.* You
can judge for yourself if you can catch them at some midnight
showing.

Romantically speaking, I did what I'd done before, slipping
into the role of the other woman to older men, only now I was
twenty-five and the dynamic felt more brittle than it once had.
My needs were supplemented with gifts bought on men's lines
of credit.

I kept myself beautiful with creams and a curling iron, shop-
lifted nail lacquer, and new calisthenics techniques Suzanna
showed me. Whenever I got rejected for something I bought
things to compensate. I filled bags with luxury groceries for
Suzanna. I gave her a bouquet of flowers and a bottle of perfume as
if she was my girlfriend. This is just to thank you for taking me in
when I was desperate. She said, you know I love it, doll, but stop
throwing your money around like an idiot. Bottles of Arpège don't
grow on trees.

One evening at a party downtown I was talking to Bobby, a tall
and skinny assistant director whom I liked but didn't know well,
when death showed itself once again.

Bobby said, oh I have some gossip that may interest you. Lev Samara's wife died. I know you worked with him a few years back and maybe it was different, but from what I've heard he is an inveterate womanizer. Supposedly he was even out with an actress when it happened. Was seen at a bar downtown that night. He was in a frenzy then, editing a film called *Farewell Performance*. I haven't seen it, but a friend did and he said the rough cut was fantastic. There are questions about who's going to distribute it.

After that I thought about Lev and Grace for days. I knew how much he had taken her for granted, but also how much he'd relied on her. I wrote him a letter saying how sorry I was. I know what it is to lose like that.

Lev's wife was indeed alone when she collapsed in their bathroom, among the pink towels with satin edgings. Their children were away at their boarding schools. Lev discovered her there when he arrived home drunk at four in the morning.

It was a brain aneurysm. There had been no warning signs except that she sometimes had bad headaches. How could Lev have known? But he should have, he said. He should have insisted she go to a specialist. She was always so blasé about her own well-being, while always worrying over others. He was inconsolable at the hospital they said, useless to his children who were there too.

Mary Grace Samaras, née Mixon, died at Manhattan's Presbyterian Hospital, never having revived after her episode. She was thirty-nine years old and was survived by her husband, their two children, and her loving parents.

On a May evening, Lev called. He was in Athens. I could hear how drunk and far he was through the crackle in the line. What time is it there? He mumbled, dark. You have a way with details, I said. Don't be a smart-ass, he said. I don't need that so much.

I sat on Suzanna's floor at the end of the telephone's cord and watched the sun set on New Jersey. The room went all edges and lines as it dimmed, slices of shadow and a black hole for a bedroom doorway. I never got up to turn on the lights. Lev cried about Grace, about his children, but he also cried about other people and things he'd seen with his own eyes like his father dead and lying in a satin-lined casket.

Lev said his daughter didn't shed a tear on the day of her mother's funeral. That's not normal, he said. But he could also understand. She has a coldness in her. I remembered my mother's memorial flowers, those purple spears of gladiolas. I said, it will be okay for her someday. Not now, but after a long while. All you can offer her is love. That's it. I have it, but I don't know if she'll want the battered kind of love I have. Her mother was the one who could be kind.

Are you sleeping enough? Are you drinking water, Lev? He said he couldn't sleep at all. I wish I could hold you. I know it's all fucked but that time in the village was quite special to me. I believed in the art we were making. I started crying myself.

After a sharp inhale Lev asked, why don't you come here? I'll buy you a ticket. What the hell, darling. Just come here and be with me and we can make each other happy for a while.

People usually did what Lev asked them to and I was a person so I went. He wired me money. I went to a travel agency and the lady booked me on a TWA 707 from JFK to Athens with stopovers in Paris and Rome. As I was packing Suzanna said, he must want you a lot to bring you all that way.

The navy-gray Atlantic rippled in gaps between the clouds. I had a coffee and croissant in Orly before going up again above the northern weather. I washed my armpits and sprayed perfume all over in the plane toilet. The air stewardess announced our descent into Athens.

Women were waving handkerchiefs from the observation deck overlooking where the planes landed. The airport was a modern city gate where banners flapped and tears were shed. *Αναχώρηση* said the signs. The sky was blue, the clouds white, and the air dry like the high desert. I walked down the stairs into the foreign heat feeling famous, like the Rolling Stones on tour. Sunglasses on and a scarf tied over my mess of hair.

When I was spit out into the crowd on the other side of customs, I spotted Lev right away. International and at home. Here his features made sense, he belonged among these people. I was happy but I could tell right away he was annoyed. He pulled me toward the throng of jockeying taxis.

During the long cab ride, he was cool. He regretted everything and it had only just begun. I'm not angry with you but at myself. I've been on a binge. Drinking too much. Working too much, he sighed.

You invited me here, I said. Can't we make the best of it? I stroked his hand and reassured him. We could pretend, like you said. I'll leave soon enough. Let me take care of you for a bit. I was so very tired.

The city grew older the deeper into the center we went. On the narrow street of dirty marble, men were gathered outside a café within billows of smoke. Their round tables were painted vivid green. The cab squeezed by, practically grazing the chairs, but no one paid it any mind. Orange and pink bougainvillea grew out of pots. These have become my favorite plants over time, with their flower petal paper leaves.

Lev's place had a few pieces of elegant antique furniture but he had no bed, just an unmade mattress covered with mismatched blankets and pillows. His sheets smelled of sweat. His skin smelled of tobacco and herbal cologne, his neck soap clean under the white collar of his shirt. I'd crossed seas to bury my face there. He pushed into me roughly. Oh God. A car honked its way through the alley street. I reached my hand back and caressed the sun-faded velvet of a curtain. Music and talk floated up from below. After we were through, he broke into stifled sobs with his head jammed into a pillow. I petted. I stroked. I pulled Lev into kissing. Baby. It's okay, baby. Anything to bring him back to the moment.

Part of acting is creating conditions that you yourself can believe in. It's convincing yourself the situation is real enough. We were survivors left to act out living, so that's what we did. The shame made things more technicolor. Lev's suffering made the honey so sweet.

I invented a character and based her on my grandmother. I had only seen my grandmother a handful of times but had heard her described many times in repeating fragments.

She immigrated to the United States from Germany because she'd been ruined by a young man named Lukas. In New York, unwed, she gave birth to my mother. I feel like they don't call girls bastards the way they do boys.

After a few years of uncertainty, my grandmother married a man who delivered beer. But after not too long he was killed while working. Something spooked the Clydesdale horses, and in their fear they pushed his wagon backward. Someone shrieked. Her husband's cracked chest seeped his whole shirt red.

My grandmother carried on, she moved west with a friend, dragging my little girl mother behind. She married again to a veteran of the first war who had problems, old ones and ones he created for himself. It was with him that my grandmother's real troubles began.

Despite her all-too-common tribulations, my grandmother was always well turned out. She applied makeup expertly, powdered her rosy décolleté, buffed her nails. She learned shorthand to be a secretary and knew all the popular dances. She was beautiful and a real charmer.

She had arrived by ship with her name written on the side of a leather suitcase. Her life could fit into that case and she was strong enough to lift it. She knew the sound of lapping against a ship's side, the look of rust-colored oil swirling at the surface of the water around a dock.

I have had so much. My grandmother could not fathom the luxury I've frittered away.

For my whole life I would take anything I could get. I know it's easy to judge me then for sleeping with a newly dead woman's husband, for having him too when she was alive. I was selfish and grotesque. I know. I have always been ashamed of what I wanted, ashamed of all the wants I had.

When Lev and I regarded one another, we had the dead between and within us. They recognized one another. It had been true from the start and was even more true when we met in Athens. I could feel these wives and ancestors, prisoners and bomb victims inside looking out.

There she goes, they murmured, shopping for groceries for another woman's husband. There he is, making coffee in a foreign home. What right have they to live their lives so? They spill and mope and flounder. They don't listen to us when we speak.

It was only my mother who didn't chatter. In silence, she watched the movies I was making. I could feel her eyes on me in the dark auditorium of Lev's borrowed apartment but I could not hear her voice.

In the mornings I went out as my character to acquire whatever was needed for the day, tomatoes and cucumbers, figs and cheese. For bigger shopping trips Lev relied on a local woman. I just played around. The vegetables there were the best I'd ever had. I wanted for the first time ever to actually eat. The food tasted vital and clean.

I picked up Sante cigarettes in their pleasing red packs. I got a heap of news from the stand that stocked international papers. *The New York Times* said Lincoln Center was getting artworks by Calder and Moore. The Hollies' "I'm Alive" was number one on the British charts. An Italian had won the Tour de France. The women of *Paris Vogue* looked out at me with pleased half smiles.

I spent my time and Lev's liras browsing for esoteric trifles. I bought a sheer embroidered nightgown and ordered a pair of sandals to be made custom for me by an old man who caressed my foot when he traced it.

In the afternoons I read while Lev worked. He laughed on long calls behind his closed door. It was always a producer or an investor on the other end. Lev flattered and exclaimed in an effort to get whatever it was he wanted to win, an invitation, a job, a chunk of change. That's a fantastic idea, Lev said. I love it. I knew he didn't because he'd told me beforehand it was garbage.

We'd eat and drink. I'd pull my skirt up and sit on his lap and we'd kiss and kiss. I'd fall asleep then half wake to feel him getting out of bed in the dark heat. He worked all hours. These overheated days never put a dent in his energy whereas I lay groggy and tangled in the sheet until late each morning.

I'd pull myself up eventually and start the ritual play again. I skimmed the leftover news with my first coffee. Lev would be returning from a stroll with layered pastries filled with a barely sweet cheese. He said a great painter had died yesterday and people were sad about it. Imagine being such an artist you're mourned at the bakery.

I found enough energy to repair the apartment's disorder. I aired out the bedroom as I smoked my first cigarette. I was a sophisticate and smelled like I slept in sprays of Fracas because I did.

Lev's friend Peter was arriving from Rome. We were having a dinner party in his honor. I draped a tablecloth and arranged a bouquet. As Lev bathed, I poured Campari into glasses and put potato chips and olives into separate bowls. I thought, sun-stroked, about the kaleidoscope possibility of films. Eyes shot up close, reflections of people caught over the shoulder. How shooting someone in a mirror enables the viewer to see front and back in a single image.

I admired things as they were. It made me happy to look. The white flowers with their black centers bowed in their brown vase atop the shrouded table in the middle of the room. The table stood beside a black-edged window that was open to a faded blue sky that stretched above a complex blocky jumble of rooftops. Singing was coming from the record player. I tested the density of a green olive between my teeth and the salt brightened all my senses. The yellow potato chips were translucent with oil. A crystal of ice was melting into the red transparency in my glass. The tiles beneath my feet were rust colored, the walls chalk white. The hills of the city were going dark blue. Each substance was itself. Things were present in my attention without them needing me. But I was there to see the light change and it moved me, giving a physical, total pleasure.

This is why we need film, because it would never be just like this again.

When Peter burst through the door he and Lev caught one another in a bear hug. They swayed and laughed and embraced and it made me emotional seeing such manly joy. Peter brought with him a whole party.

The men talked about bombing campaigns and riots, Visconti and Powell while the women listened. Women I hadn't ever met flickered in eggshell blue and mimosa, pure red and onyx, and silver. Not because we didn't have opinions on bigger things, but because it was easier, we complimented one another's hair and perfumes.

There were more men than women and the words poured mostly from the men's mouths. I didn't mind. It was relaxing to hear the history of the present tumble out in arguments and off-color jokes. They talked about uprising and box office numbers, fascists who'd gotten away with everything and were still in control. They talked about women they thought were especially beautiful, islands they wanted us all to visit, and sex they wanted us all to have. This was surely the collapse of something the men agreed.

The local woman often cooked for Lev, when he had people over. She always kept me out of the kitchen during her preparations. But she was old and went home to cook for her husband before the parties began.

Peter's girlfriend Olivia and I took turns choosing records. She'd even brought some new things with her. I made vodka tonics. I doused the salad with lemon and oil. Then we had lamb and rice that people barely ate. There was wine and we drank it all. We served the limoncello someone brought from duty-free. The custard pie no one wanted but we had it on hand to be good hosts. I poured coffee into thin china cups glazed red, then offered more alcohol.

Girls, forget the cleaning, Lev said. But we couldn't. None of us liked leaving things a mess. Olivia helped me and we laughed about nothings and danced around as we did dishes.

Come outside and look at the view. Look at the Acropolis under the full moon. We are so lucky to be here in this beautiful world. Play another record, they asked, and we chose. Finally, when it was so late it had circled back to early, the guests said they had to go. And then Lev said come to bed and I did.

I had grown up drinking milk or water out of glasses I was careful not to break. I was a careful child and cool neutral drinks were the only thing that touched my throat and inner body. My father drank water, weak coffee in the morning, maybe a token bottle of beer on Friday night, or a symbolic whiskey when it was some meaningful day like the end of the war. He was controlled and did not care for the heavy stuff he said. In my family alcohol was the spirit that possessed others, so it was exotic for me to make my way into the fray of clubs and nightcaps and tying one on. Lev had a drink for any time of day and every season, and yet he drank a style that was the opposite of vulgar. Burning liquors made of exotic herbs and pristine grains went down throats. Out of them came endearments and shouts and wild ideas. Lev and Peter and all the men they liked so much said sweetheart and darling. They said, my angel can you get us another, and it relaxed me, hearing that.

My father never had this rhythm. Women and wine, they simply had not occurred to my father as issues, as pleasures or pursuits. Flattery and endearment were not logical to him. He could not treat women with anything beyond cordial disinterest, and that extended even to my mother. So, this warmth Lev expressed could tint even the most mundane interaction with an erotic hue. Blue afternoons under an arbor. Nights by the sea under a yellow light.

If you haven't grown up with them, men who drink and laugh and sing and love their friends, you find them the most irresistible kind in the whole world. At least that's how it has been for me.

I love being called honey because it feels plush like a hotel robe. I couldn't feel guilty for giving in to the pleasures of sexual suggestion because it felt nourishing, rehydrating after an early life of austerity.

I called Lev daddy in bed. Is it too magazine-psychotherapy, easy to conjure fathers and directors when analyzing a woman's proclivities? Just because it's easy doesn't mean it's unimportant. I wanted what my father wasn't. I wanted what my mother didn't choose. I wanted someone to tell me what to do. I had to restart my heart somewhere. One needs allies to get by. Lev always said that. You can't survive in this world without a rabbi. It's common sense, he said. Who would you be without friends and lovers?

I was supposed to leave. Lev was supposed to go in a different direction. That was supposed to be the end of it. I was a foreigner passing through my lover's ancient land. He said let's go to the beach one more time. My head is pounding and salt water is medicinal.

Grab your suit, he said.

The car he'd borrowed crept down the street to a barrage of honks. Hands waved out rolled-down windows. Go around for Christ's sake. The weather was still summer but it was turning.

At the beach we settled next to a gaggle of seagulls. These birds had a great careless way of standing like they had nowhere to be, but were also waiting for something vital. They were waiting to steal our potato chips, Lev scoffed.

We went out into the green waves. I kept jumping and floating with the swells, doing my best to avoid getting smacked to the face. I tried not to be afraid in the water, but I always was a little. Maybe it was a consequence of growing up in the mountains. Lev swam out far and then right back in a short athletic burst. Out of breath he said he needed a cigarette and strode back to shore.

We were lounging on our beach towels, propped up on our elbows and facing the sea when Lev asked out of the blue, what the hell, do you want to get married? Let's go back to New York and be done with it. I laughed. But I don't have the right dress. So, buy something, dummy. It's not so complicated.

The clothing of my memory shifts around, like a skirt twisted so that the zipper's over my hip when it's supposed to be in the back. I try smoothing myself out but my layers hinder. Beneath the skirt my tights, then underwear against my skin.

Before I was in this western film, my father died. Before that I was hypnotized by a vampire. Some long time ago I was a young woman, a girl. My mother died then.

You can't call yourself an orphan at forty, that would be ridiculous. Everyone's parents are either dead or alive, so it's nothing special really.

My father thought, because he was empirical, there were just two options, like a light switch. A person can be dead or alive. Additionally, I guess, is the branching possibility of knowing or not. You know if someone is alive or dead, or you don't.

I know who my parents were, give or take. I know when they each died, factually speaking. But in this line, as with so much, I diverge from my father's thinking. A person can be both alive and dead. We dress in layers of mortality. That's how it feels to me.

Soon I'm expected on set where I will lie in a bed and smoke pretend opium for a while, until we have it just right. I have my petticoat and stockings, camisole and bloomers, my blouse and skirt and boots to change into. All the layers are draped over a chair waiting for me.

The curtains blow out the propped-open window. In the late afternoon sunbeams, pines, and aspens sway. The forest makes its sound of being rocked gently by the wind. I admire it as I change.

Jet-lagged and sun-stroked, Lev and I got married. I wore something lacy, bought off the rack from the summer sale section.

After that I moved right away into his apartment.

I wondered if I'd made a mistake getting remarried, and under these circumstances. Just the scale of Lev's apartment made me nervous. Walking around from room to room I kept thinking I'd meet the dead I'd sensed in Greece. Was Grace here or had she gone? Was my mother watching the spectacle I'd become? Did I have an audience here?

I was not Lev's new housewife, but I was not *not* her. I was still an actress but I did tidy up because if it was left to Lev, overflowing ashtrays would stink up the whole place. Grace must have done so much. I'd sweep and scrub and toss bags down the chute before a real professional came on Fridays to clean properly.

I felt guilty. The cleaning lady and I were in the positions we were in because of class and chance, cheekbones and crystallized power. I was here because Lev chose. But what did the cleaning lady care about my guilt? I'd add more money to her tip envelope and go out. Leave her to work in peace.

I went to Bloomingdale's and bought a new towel set and shower curtain for the master bath, the room where Grace collapsed. Her spirit did whatever was the opposite of haunting. I never felt anything spooky in there but an absence, an achy loneliness.

The brilliance of the vanity mirror's lights created a black void in the reflection. I considered repainting but never did. The new towels were printed with red roses and the shower curtain was covered with pink butterflies, which I read symbolized the soul.

Lev's apartment would be empty for a time and then fill, like a field where migrating birds settled for a night before taking off again. Sometimes I was lonely and walked around barefoot on the plush rugs, listening to the breezes and the honking of the automobiles on the congested corner below. Then, one of Lev's children, Michael or Iris, would arrive with their well-bred frustrations.

They still had their rooms but came home only with a heavy dragging of feet. Michael was in his junior year at Amherst and Iris was about to leave for a year abroad at École Normale Supérieure. From them I learned the import of these schools. My own lack of education was poked at. I was hopelessly soft. Had I heard of Elias Canetti? What about Henri Lefebvre? I tried to avoid embarrassment but found it regardless. I said I mostly read plays and fiction. Iris rolled her eyes blatantly. I sometimes gave Michael some extra spending money. He thanked me but also stole things from my purse. I think just to show me he could. Iris would never ask for a thing and refuse whatever I offered. I heard her crying sometimes behind her closed bedroom door. I told her once I'd lost my mother too. She dismissed that. It wasn't the same. The same could be said for any two deaths. Nothing was the same as anything else.

The phone rang often. People came by seeking Lev's advice. They needed him. He provided. I was not complaining, for I too belonged to the line of supplicants. But at least I was grateful. Whatever he gave, whatever check he picked up or bill he paid, people asked afterward, is that all? Perhaps I just resented being so far down the pecking order. One among the flock.

I picked up the phone and it was Lev's mother. He wasn't home. She wanted to make plans for the holiday. Could I write a note? She was worried about the children. Have him call back.

Lev swept in and kissed me with his coat still on, squeezed my ass so I felt special. Then he was on to the next things, folding himself a sandwich out of whatever was in the fridge and dragging the phone over to his lounge chair. Don't worry about dinner, he said. I hadn't been if we were honest.

The maroon velvet chair cocooned him. He lit a cigarette. Ensconced, he dialed. Voices on the other end of the line gave their reports; they entertained. He listened and expounded, laughed and cajoled. He'd get up and pace, then change rooms. The cord snaked around corners and under doors. He'd shut himself in his office sometimes and then I could only make out his murmuring end of these endless conversations.

All right, I was jealous because I was childish, his girl. But, conversely, I also wanted him to choose them, to favor his projects, his family, his secrets over me because I could then be alone.

A psychotherapist once commented that my avoidance was more about my own childhood than about Lev, but then wouldn't elaborate. He said he'd said too much. Of course, my hang-ups are about my mother and father. That's what they always say. But never mind.

We made frequent pilgrimages to Lev's family home out on Long Island. It was a two-story, pitched-roof place made of white boards and flanked by nice trees that changed color appropriately with each season. Port Washington looked like the America I'd always seen in magazines but never exactly lived in. It was not the logs and denim west or the smokestack and money city, but a nice American town with porches and lawns and views of the sea.

In one sense Lev's family home was just as it appeared to be. A modest dwelling visited by relatives on holidays. There were countless homes just like it all over their town and really, the whole East Coast. Yet, I came to know it was also something else, a portal, an outpost of a homeland that no longer existed anywhere except in Lev's family's group mind. This place on Hillview Ave. was a way station where the saddest women I've ever met came together to drink glasses of homemade liquors that tasted of bitter herbs. They gathered there because they could not return to their true home, no matter if their papers were in order.

As soon as we arrived Lev would abandon me to fend for myself with the womenfolk. The rules and activities were split according to marital status and gender. Lev and his kids went straight to the den where the old men and youth camped out with the TV and the hi-fi.

I was a permanent outsider yet expected to stay and make efforts that would fail. Without Lev to translate all I had the courage to do was listen and fold napkins.

The women in Lev's family were many and I always saw them together. His mother had seven sisters. Five were still alive, four lived in New York, and each had experienced baroque tribulation.

Food had been prepared for three days prior. Stories were being retold with great care, not for new listeners but for the survival of the speaker. The other relatives knew when to hum and sigh. Soldiers were beating strikers with their batons, Lev's aunt said. I saw them chasing some boys who'd been playing ball. Then a soldier shot one and there was pandemonium. People in the village had been starving for that whole terrible season. It got worse and worse and I remember my mother hiding us when soldiers came to the door. When we had to leave, we slept standing up, delirious and leaning up against one another enough to relax. We slept sitting on waiting room benches to keep our place in line. Yes, I remember, another aunt said.

There was chicken and a roast; boiled greens; pastries with chocolate; creams mixed with flowers.

The women progressed to details of who suffered and who died recently. Tuesday would be his name day. It's not something I forget. The speaker daubed her eyes. Garlic she said. Remember Sara's sister Emma? The government made her wait three and a half years for her papers and in the meantime Petros died. She had to come the long way through. She was in Hong Kong. It's a wonder she survived. Where is she now? In Long Beach with her son. I got a letter.

Because of the aunts there also existed daughters who ranged in age. The older ones powdered and rouged themselves, the younger ones were still older than me. One said I should fix my hair. Another said she admired me being a modern woman and not caring what people thought of my clothes. She had a bright red manicure. A bit of pâté stuck to her fingertips when she dipped some bread. I restrained a shudder.

I reacted to the heat and food and stories by becoming mute as I usually did. Sadness emanated from them in rays. It slid through my cells, disrupting them like radiation. No matter how much sadness came from them, there was always more. I lost all appetite. I asked if there was something else I could do.

Will you put out the silverware, dear? We'll sit down to supper soon. Lev's mother patted my shoulder and said, we're glad you're here, we just want Lev's happiness.

Men and children lolled in the living room around the television that was set to silent football. In the den, this clan's contemporary youth were listening to the radio. Is this a dream, Dionne Warwick asked in her song while the kids laughed at some intra-cousin jokes.

I circled the dining table made long with its temporary wings, distributing silverware and the embroidered napkins, folded all nice. On-screen, the Trojans were hammering the Hoosiers in sunny Pasadena.

When I wanted to hide in Lev's apartment, I'd go to the second bathroom that was beside the spare room that had belonged to a maid in the olden days. Lev called it the maid's room even though no maid had slept in it for a long time.

I liked blowing smoke out this absent maid's bathroom window. It looked out into a non-view of the communal air shaft. When finished I'd drop my spent Lucky Strikes out the window. Though I couldn't see all the way down, I liked the image in my mind's eye of the heap of crumpled butts gathering on the roof. They were a growing monument to each day I spent as a second wife.

I relaxed best in the bathroom enclosure. I'd read scripts to the faint sounds of other people peeing. I'd fix my eyebrows and massage my temples. I'd pluck hairs and paint toenails. Sometimes I'd take a bath in there, even though all my oils and scrubbers were in the master. Phones rang in other apartments. Neighbors had sex or raised their voices to one another in complaint. Our close strangeness echoed. The shaft was an inside-out tower, built for light and air but not for a view. At its core was a void, and facing that empty space is where I could sink into thoughts about things I didn't normally like to think about, such as my mother.

———

My mother.

She could have been a star if they'd let her. On the screen, yes, but also the kind in the sky. A star is a kind of astral bomb going off, only slower, its twinkling is the light and heat of atoms joining. What we see, in our short human lives, are blips in cosmic time. Stars burn brightest, they make one last effort to keep shining right before they die. My father told me all that, not about my mother, but about physics. Of her, he had much less to say.

My mother had beautiful cheekbones and the right kind of outer stillness for the screen. Her chemical reactions went on internally so that you didn't know they were happening till it was too late. She could have been something bigger but her timing was wrong. She had all sorts of things that got in the way of her own natural potential: miscarriages and interminable train trips, western union telegrams and a mother who needed to borrow money, bad water coming from bad taps, and me as a baby in a red sweater, crying. Despite her promise, my mother was just one more obscure beauty, sitting in a military base canteen, staring at the beige hamburger on a plate in front of her feeling everything but hungry.

My mother held my hand as we walked through a grocery store. She was dressed in her green coat with its fur collar. She said we'd make something special, a cake. Her voice lilted while talking to the man stocking the shelves. She wanted the best. But sorry ma'am. We don't have any cream or currants. We don't have cherries, even canned, and we don't have lady fingers. We left with a can of Postum, a square white loaf of bread, and butter that was margarine. She made me a piece of cinnamon sugar toast once we got home and nothing more was said about cake.

How did mothering make my mother feel? I think she wanted something other than that. But still, she was pregnant more times than me, though the other times didn't become real. Maybe my unborn brothers and sisters would have made her happier, but probably not. I remember her putting a saint card on her dresser beside her bouquet of crepe paper flowers. I remember her often being sad. I know when she was little some things happened.

A man can ruin a child, no problem. A man can ruin a child for decades or even for their whole life and the man could be so drunk he doesn't even realize he's doing it. Or maybe that's the point of the drunkenness, not to know what they're doing. Carelessness, meanness, tangled-up want, can be so easy and yet their consequences reverberate out and out. Like a blast wave. Like a ripple. The child has been given the elements of trust and disgust. Hot breath in a small bed. Just between us he said. The gleam of wet teeth in the dark. I know in that indefinite time of American crisis, in the age of her childhood, my mother was hurt like that. She was irradiated in her own room, where she was supposed to be safe. How many years did my mother remain factually alive while internally her cells were damaged, while inside she was dying? How many times did the father figure smother her? There was the harm he did to her physically, and also what he did to her mind, her memories. How many times did the film play? In the intimacy of flannel sheets how many times did he press away her air while the glass of water on the bedside table stood by and didn't even quiver?

I wonder, I can't help it, if it was that hurt or what came later that caused her death. Was it me, or the father figure, or the war, or my father and his work, or all, in accumulation? Why not all? Why "no but" and not "yes and"?

I remember my mother weeping over pages in magazines, a photograph of the bomb detonating, a ball of fire. This was my father's work. This, they say, is what ended the war. I can't bear it, my mother said. Her friend Renata replied, but bearing it is the only choice, honey. I've always thought, when I'm blue, Renata said, that if you kill yourself your soul remains trapped on earth until the rightful time when God intended for you to die.

When once I asked what happened, my father said this: When the bomb falls, everything and everyone within the immediate blast, the earth and the water, the people and animals that were just before whole, becomes a vapor. This is what makes a mushroom cloud. Radioactive stuff mixes with the dust of everything that burned. After the initial intense, unthinkably hot heat, the cloud begins to cool and all that was vapor condenses and falls back to earth. This radioactive dust contaminates whatever it lands on. When a bomb goes off people who aren't immediately incinerated are squeezed by a great pressure. Their internal organs rupture. A blast sends these broken bodies through the air.

Whoever is burned instantly is lucky in a way, because their death occurs faster than the mind can process. The people who are farther away are blinded, either temporarily, or forever. With radiation poisoning, my father said that even the littlest thing could mean the difference between death and survival. Dropping flat and covering your eyes, hiding what exposed skin you can. There are ways to survive an atomic blast, my father said, but I wonder sometimes if he said that to give me something to hope for, in the event of a catastrophe.

My mother was so sad. She was sad enough to leave me and the world and now I can do nothing but remember her.

One Sunday there is a day off from shooting the western, so Jake and I lie in bed without worrying about the time. Feeling blurry I try to describe to him my mother and how she made me feel.

She comes to me sometimes, I said. And when she comes, she uses me like a hotel. I become the Eldorado. I go when she arrives. I can't ever question her because I scurry away.

It's possible to think about pain quite often without ever getting closer to understanding it. My mother visits me without me knowing her. I leave. I return. I leave again. The scent of other women's perfume lingers in the hall. I can't fill myself with myself. I move around as if in a trance.

The film *Les Diaboliques*, have you seen it? In it a wife and a mistress collaborate to murder the man they have in common. They want his end because he is cruel to them both. But then, after it's done, the wife is guilt ridden and she feels that her dead husband has returned to haunt her. There are strange occurrences. She discovers a hotel room rented in his name and inside the empty room she finds the suit he was wearing when he died, back from the cleaner, just hanging behind the door. He has been in, the concierge tells her, but the bed is never slept in. The wife goes bit by bit insane as she churns through the supernatural possibilities and their implications.

I recognize myself in that wife looking in horror at the empty black suit, as it hangs beside a mirror that reflects back her face.

Picture an empty bedroom with pale floral wallpaper. The room leads to a bathroom and the door is open, you can see through the frame the implements of care and cleanliness arranged on the counter. Toothbrushes and paste, a bottle of Bay Rum, and a shaker of talcum powder. In the mirror's reflection there's a ceramic cup and inside the cup a silver safety razor loaded with a fresh blade. You can find deadly weapons anywhere if you have the will to look.

My life is unspooling this way, without me knowing my past or myself. I do not know how to act like a person. But perhaps it's this vacancy that makes me a good actress. I wonder if art has to do with my desperation? I can be filled at a moment's notice. I can be filled up for one night or weeks at a time. People can meet one another and fuck inside me, discreetly, without their spouses knowing. I provide a Continental breakfast and a turndown service.

Do you think if I become happier and begin to understand myself, I'll lose all my talent?

Jake adjusted his arm so that it made a pillow. Honey, was all he could say. I let the feel of his warm skin sink into me and make me warm too.

The only useful thing I know how to do when I'm not working is audition and study.

Lying in the park with Suzanna I'd memorize monologues. Sometimes I'd have pages for a part I was going for. With whatever I had I'd write up notes about the meanings that lay beneath the words. I love interpretation.

If I had some pages for an audition Suzanna and I would invent backstories with heartache and intensity. This character has just learned her mother has died when she enters this scene. She's a paranoiac and worries a man has been following her. She's throwing herself at this detective sexually because he represents safety and order. That's why she acts this way.

More often than not, the material I had to work with could not bear the weight of our blue-sky preparations. The women I wanted to play were not generally the ones on offer.

I showed up at the casting agents' offices. In those hushed waiting rooms there sat other blondes like me, foreign and domestic, some taller, others more petite, many younger. We were all made up like cover girls. All we assembled blondes could hope for was winning the prize role of the alluring journalist in glasses who sleeps with the detective because he's irresistible. Another time, if we were the lucky one, we'd get to portray the jaded girlfriend who was dumped for the incandescent teenager. No one wants to know the subtle backstory of why your character is the way she is, but sure, if it's fun, invent something. Go to town.

They'd call my name and I'd smooth my skirt and undo another button so that they could see down my blouse but not in an obvious way. Today you'll be reading for the flirty neighbor with a dark past. I was paired with a gaunt and menacing stranger. It wasn't clear if he had the role yet. The casting agent and the director watched. We tried the pages casual. Can you go again but give it all you got. You're taking it too seriously. Try fun and flirtier, the director requested. This character you see, he's a deviant without even noticing. He'd choke you as soon as look at you. Maybe he actually likes to look at you choking. You'd be the third girl he attacks, but your character escapes while the others die. At first, she's excited, but then it turns. Could you do it with that in mind, just one more time? I'd love to.

They would reach out, call, let me know. So many assurances I knew nothing would come to me. The next girl was out in the hall already. The next day, or weeks later, the phone would ring and it would be my agent on the other end, all soothing tones and we'll-get-'em-next-time promises. They thought you were something special but went in another direction.

———

When I wasn't working on my acting, I went to movies. I went to all of them. I watched films shot at Paramount and Cinecittà, at Elstree in England, and on Bergman's Island of Fårö. I saw big pictures with Jack Nicholson made in British Columbia, and strange singular things shot in Cairo. I watched in the plush red subterranean caverns of Lincoln Plaza Cinema and while sweating on a folding chair downtown at Film Forum. I loved to be in the audience. At a gallery I saw a film by a compatriot of Picasso. I sat in the dark beside all the artists. In black and white, nude women disappeared behind curtains while men gambled. The roulette wheel spun. Players eyed one another across a poker table.

Here was a film about a woman who loses her mind then drowns her child. She saw no other options. Most of the film takes place in a courtroom after the fact. Could the jury understand the conditions that led to such an act?

There was a B movie about a mass killer perched in a bell tower, just like Charles Whitman. I read in the paper at the time how he killed both his mother and wife with knives before climbing up those stairs with his gun. He got a sharpshooter badge from the Marines, the papers reported as a footnote. In the movie, the character is apprehended, he doesn't commit suicide. His rampage makes him a star. The news cameras love him. He has a bunch of groupies.

I gorged on movies about war and its aftermath. There were the guilty and the innocent, the spared and the cut down.

Languages mingled. Sound effects mismatched subtlety. I drifted through a matinee. Once one film ended, I walked across the hall. High production value, well-considered cinematography made it all go down easy. There was the rough and then the smooth with each episode flowing naturally in the next. Schlesinger and Teshigahara, Pietri and Lean, any films can make a double feature if you just keep watching.

There was a film where two women played one character. Her lover saw her as split between prudish virgin and untrustworthy vixen. The two actresses played the one role's body, but I learned from an article that the voice belonged to a third woman, who we never saw. I read also another, fourth woman had been cast to play the whole character but she'd left, perhaps been fired from the production because she was too wild. I remembered her curly hair and fallen-angel face and thought to myself, she is the true actress. The greatest performance is sometimes by the absent woman, the one we don't see but only imagine.

I sat in the audience watching the actresses hovering in double exposure. I always watch women more closely, even though men are generally the characters with the most to do. The women are all too often deluding themselves into something awful. They know a trap when they see one but it doesn't mean they won't step right into the steel jaws. The women were alone even when clinging arm and arm with a best friend. Their allure could turn grotesque or sinister, tragic or pathetic, and I loved them for those turns. Some asked if there would come a time when they could stop suffering just because they'd been born women. All this was rarely stated but it was there. I could see it.

When I'd get back to Lev's apartment I'd write in my journal and it made as much sense as this. I cataloged the things I knew. Those things I didn't know were too many to innumerate.

I crossed the plaza in front of Lincoln Center. The water shooting up and arcing back down in its black marble enclosure did much to drown out traffic noise. I imagined myself beside a temple spring.

Only in a few locales in the city could you get the feel of a ruin, of the austerity we associate with the Greeks. Across the way, framed by the high-rises of regular time, green leaves fluttered in afternoon light.

I got to the park, spread my blanket on the lawn, and kicked off my shoes. I never wore hose because I had come to hate their false tawny sheen. Sheer black tights in winter I like because they announce themselves, they're not trying to hide their artifice.

In summer I want my legs bare even though they're marked by the scars I've made by picking at myself with tweezers. This is an obsessive habit I have. I lose so much time doing this while hidden in the bathroom. I think about my mother when I pluck. I twist myself into odd angles until my back aches. I soothe myself with pain. I know it's bad, but I can't stop. My legs are continually pock-marked in a half-healing, half-irritated state. I paint my toenails to distract and they shimmer like shells at the end of my body.

Suzanna arrived with wine and plastic picnic cups, watermelon and potato chips. The expanse of public green was brown in areas from the heat. Some people strolled while others zigzagged as they tossed Frisbees. Still others made static configurations; gaggles of friends smoked grass in the grass, sunbathing girls quilted the lawn with their blanket squares. They flipped the magazine pages as their thighs turned golden. Rock music from tinny transistors filled the humid air.

It used to be I'd use this time to analyze people, study the scene to use it for acting, but since the last rejection my mind has been fluttering like a paperback in the breeze. I'd been feeling lazy.

Suzanna wanted to tell me the story of her recent trip, she'd just returned from the Keys for what turned out to be a disastrous visit to a man she'd thought she was in love with. She'd been crazy about this man for months and he'd finally invited her down to his bungalow. But now it was all over.

The first night was charmed: pink orange light and a pearlescent sea, shrimp boats rocking to and fro to the music of the clapboard bar's band. She put a plumeria behind her ear. It was the whole bit, a regular postcard. But then, after they'd made love and she'd fallen asleep fantasizing about the life they'd lead, Suzanna woke to a terrible sensation all over her body. When she leapt up, scratching, almost crying, her beau was laconic. He explained it was a kind of plant pollen that blew in through the window. Take a shower, he said. If you're down here long enough you get used to it. He swore it had never bothered him, maybe he was immune. Suzanna tossed and itched all night, enveloped in the most torturous irritation.

I'd met Suzanna's man when he was in the city visiting. He was silver white on the head and deep tan everywhere else from boating. He'd made his money as a chemist in Nutley, New Jersey, but then divorced and transformed into a man of leisure down south. We'd all eaten shish kebab together downtown. Lev's opinion was that Stan wasn't a serious person. Perhaps he was one of those having a midlife crisis like the magazines described. Suzanna had told me Stan talked about marriage and was oh so serious with her, so I didn't know whose word to take.

The next morning, they went for a swim and there again, adding insult to itchiness, Suzanna was stung when a jellyfish tendril wrapped her calf. She became hysterical out in the surf, blubbering and staggering as she tried to escape the alien sting. Stan had to drag-carry her out. This was God speaking to her, she thought, but still, she didn't listen. No, she told herself, these were just anomalies, vulnerable freak occurrences that were pushing her even more into the arms of her beloved. She forged ahead.

In the afternoon, drunk on rum, Suzanna asked what Stan imagined as a future. He replied that he didn't want to be tied down. He had done the whole Plymouth in the driveway, dinner at six, and it had been murder. He thought they were lucky to experience this time of new consciousness. She was a true bohemian he thought, she had opened him up to so much spiritual, karmic awareness. She and a woman he'd met down there. He didn't want this to be the end with Suzanna but rather a fresh beginning. To be honest, he hoped the three of them could meet and explore possibilities if Suzanna was game. The other woman had seen her photo and heard everything about her.

Well, you can imagine.

Suzanna was laughing while tearing up. After a terrible fight she ended up on his porch. There was an open screen door and a long white concrete walkway reflecting the tropical light back up and all along it were green lizards soaking in the warmth. Each lizard had a throat that pulsed, miniature translucent balloons that became opaque when the air was released. The lizards puffed and relaxed while she cried and cried. Watching them, she said, put me in a trance so that eventually I wasn't thinking anymore. There was just the air with its insect sounds and the lizards with their throats. I had a desire to touch one, Suzanna said, to hold one in my hand. But the moment I made even the most careful movement in their direction, they'd scatter. I don't feel I can ever get ahold of my life, she said.

But then what happened?

Stan found a friend to drive me to Miami, they were leaving for the airport, as it turned out. *C'est la vie* sweetheart, he said. You can't have hard feelings this far south. The gall, she laughed, the audacity.

Suzanna said I shouldn't put up with Lev's infidelities. I should be the one and not one among many. But jealousy, the deep kind, is such a soap opera. "Unfaithful" is a supermarket word in my dictionary. Sometimes there's a religious aspect to Suzanna's sense of propriety that sends my eyes rolling. Maybe if you have a strictly atheist father, a suicided mother, and a grandmother banished from Germany for her sluttishness you can't not wonder if fidelity matters. Marriage as practical care stamped by City Hall means something to me. As does attention in the moments you're with your lover, but when you're apart you live in different worlds. I myself struggle not to sleep with any man who shows me some kindness.

There's nothing after this, my father said. We're a sack holding a scattering of elements. We are made mostly of oxygen followed by carbon and then roughly the same hydrogen and nitrogen. Every other element we have in such small amounts it's hardly worth tracking. We have in our bodies enough phosphorus to make a few thousand matches but only enough iron to make one medium-size nail. We have just enough magnesium to create a flash for one photograph. And even with all that interesting mystery, the puzzle that is how we are made, we've gotten twisted up with stories of angels dancing on the head of a pin. My father always scoffed whenever he came around to the problem of religion, morality, traditions. What were we living to do?

My mother, when she could, argued back. Just because something can't be reduced to chemistry doesn't mean it's not powerful. I had one parent who was scornful and defensive because he worked on the bomb and another parent who'd slit her own throat to escape the torment of her consciousness. Together they made a family. What did I care who slept with who while we were all alive?

Nihilism will ruin your soul, Suzanna said. I told her I was sorry to be so dour, and I was sad to hear about Stan. But there are loads of fantastic men in New York. Maybe I can set you up with Lev's friend Micky like I offered. She didn't want to hear it and collapsed back on our blanket in despair.

One day, in the months after I'd returned to the city after Simon Tremblay and our absurd marriage, Suzanna and I went to see a medium. I was pining for an inaccessible man I knew, for Lev, for some theoretical man I'd never encountered.

The medium saw us in her apartment in Hell's Kitchen. She didn't have the candles and spooky brocade I'd imagined but rather a nice teak table and a clean white sheepskin rug. She had a yellow fondue set displayed on a shelf. We three sat at the table and held hands. She guided us through a light hypnotism I guess only I fell under. Suzanna was disappointed. She wanted her own journey into her incarnations. I couldn't help being suscepti-ble. The medium said Suzanna's time of the month might be causing a disruption.

In my altered state I found myself as a page, a knight's boy, and who was I helping but Lev Samaras. I knew, as you understand things in dreams, that neither of us was ourselves as we are now, but still he was he, and I, I. I could hear the snap of banners over our heads, hundreds of them, blue and black and gold, creating a roar of wind in fabric. I could feel a horse between my legs. We were both spiritually devout and prepared to die together on the field. I loved him and knew we'd be separated and reunited through time. He was not just my director but a brother, my captain, my beloved. From his noble profile I could see he was a man who'd come from martyrs and jokers, revolutionaries and poets banished for their art, the kind of people who survived for the same reason they were killed through the eons. He came from a lineage of smart-asses with mystical visions. They were the kind who couldn't keep their mouths shut even knowing the cost. He'd washed up onto the shores of New York, and his clan now drove around Long Island in Cadillacs and Buicks, but we were bound by a cycle of reincarnation that rolled back to the ancients.

Lev was not as terrible as Suzanna made him out. Not by any stretch. He was fantastic, adored by so many I felt amazed he wanted me. I wanted his conviviality to rub off. I wanted the adoration he had. He had the confidence of inner circles and knowledge of far cities. Dogs, toddlers, and old women warmed under his gaze. Women melted. Old men wanted him to join their card games.

Lev encouraged me to let men touch me. He wanted to catch a glimpse of me slipping into the hall or backing into the maid's room during a party. Oh no, you're so bad but I can't help it. I learned one way to have fun was to get them to show you the impulses they keep hidden. Men who'd made some money were little fascists without even noticing. It took almost nothing to get them to reveal their desire to abuse or to be abused. Slap my face, they'd say. Spit on me. What can't a girl absorb?

Lev in his crisp, simple shirts and dark slacks was ready to push and bleed. He was a touched being who might sweep the contents of a nicely set table crashing to the floor just to remind us we were here, on this earth, today. I know it sounds awful, but he always gave off a kind of ecstatic, animated joy. It sparked off him. I knew we were bonded on an atomic level, through the ages. I found my past life love forever irresistible.

I took a bath while Lev listened to the Mets on the radio. I could hear his exclamations when both the right and the wrong things happened. A swing and a miss. A run given up. You've got to be joking, he grumbled.

We had in our fridge lean chops from the butcher, not the market. We had all the ingredients for a nice salad. We had green grapes and a carton of Neapolitan wearing a crown of ice crystals. We had a case of Rheingold, bottles of Beefeater and Stolichnaya, and even some home-brewed raki from Lev's cousin. The living room carpet had fans of vacuum impressions from the cleaner and the ashtrays smelled of liquid Dawn rather than soot, but I still said, let's go out. I don't feel like staying at home. I didn't say exactly but communicated that I wanted to be treated special, like a strange girl he'd want to impress. Of course, sweetheart, Lev agreed.

He called Peter and suddenly it was a party.

The maître d' at the restaurant knew Peter and Lev, so things were arranged before our arrival. Each dining room he led us through felt deeper and cooler than the last. It was one of the city's cigar-hazed establishments with velvet curtains, frosted-glass half walls, and filagree patterned wallpaper in the powder room. We were destined for the heart of the heart of the place where deeds were done over lobster salad.

Look over there, is that Jack with Bob and Anne? It was and it was. They came right over and acted so sweet. You're looking fantastic. Ann pouted, when will we work together? I'm waiting for a call. Lev enjoyed this flirtation happening in front of me.

I might have been the prettiest girl in Grand Junction but I was far from the smartest. Here I couldn't claim the most of anything. Women with No. 5–spritzed décolleté and patent leather nails slid by Lev all the time. There were heaps of women who'd gone to one of the seven sisters and undergone analysis and had nervous breakdowns, and LSD trips and experiences of sexual healing. They had eating disorders and reading groups. I had no college and no mother. I'd never officially fallen apart. I cried in the maid's room. I bit my nails, picked my skin in hidden places, and drank too much.

Bob asked Lev what they'd do next. Lev said he'd started writing a script about the assassination of a leftist political candidate and it would be the government, in collusion with members of the military, who carried out the killing. The story would follow both the plotters and the victim in a naturalistic style. We'd see layer after layer, the hiring of a hit man, the police abandoning their posts at a key moment, undercover agitators sowing discord between the politician's student supporters. Bankers and generals in hushed conversation. All the way up and down, we'll see what's said before news cameras and then the plotting and threats carried out in private. Our own reality will be

just there, hovering around the fiction. As Lev grew more animated Peter's head sunk lower and lower until it was resting on
the tablecloth in mock despair.

What do you have against success? Peter asked. Have you ever
thought about making something about a couple? Something
hopeful? Or even something like a simple crime picture? Have you
ever thought about making us some money?

All around other diners' voices were amplified with drink. I slid
around on our deep leather banquet, already tipsy. We laughed at
the notion of Lev's romantic comedy. A musical maybe. We howled.

I soothed myself watching Anne and Lev talk as if they were
both strangers.

When I was the mistress, I clung to Lev's arm with so much
need. It disgusted me. But now because I lived in his house I could
let go. I could be alluring in new ways. I could pull focus when
necessary, could crawl in sheer underwear across the thick carpet
to his knee and look up with fluttered lashes. Our living room
could be muffled and calm despite Amsterdam Ave traffic. I could
look up into his face and know when he needed a concentrated
moment of devotional sex.

Women wore scars like scarves of fine tissue around the neck.
I put my hands on the table.

Jack slid in beside me in the booth. He was Peter's friend. A
handsome man smelling of sandalwood. He had a business, he said,
import. Maybe that was refreshing compared to the movies. He
was just back from Boulder, Colorado. It was a rarefied part of the
state. I'd never been. He talked of a meeting with the Maharishi

Mahesh, a dinner in a canyon with a rock and roll band. Pure debauchery. One of them threw a leather couch out a third-floor window. Jack said it was the kind of beautiful furniture he would have sacrificed a limb for when he was poor. So much waste. He sighed. But the conditions are so strange now it's no wonder the young are losing their minds. The couch crashed apart when it landed on the concrete slab of the driveway, just inches away from a new Ferrari.

It was an idiotic scene if you ask me, but they did have a great wine collection. I blame that nonsense on the cocaine.

My my, I said. Did you go anywhere else in Colorado?

No, I went on to California, which was just terrific. I picked tangelos right off the trees of the house I was staying in. You can spend days barefoot, juice dripping down your chin, reading Rilke in a hammock. It's possible there to just experience the pure pleasure of life.

He stroked my shoulder, casual. Had we met before this, he asked. You look familiar. I was so drunk by that point I didn't have the discipline to explain I'd acted, was acting at the moment. I said I just had that kind of face, I guess. Someone suggested we go to a nightclub. In the front rooms chairs were up on tables and a man in a bow tie was wielding a vacuum.

We caught a cab that ferried us through Districts, Theater then Garment. I rolled down the window and let the cold air slap the spins out of me. I leaned into the breeze like a dog. I'm all out of cigarettes, Lev said, can we stop at a newsstand? And everyone said, of course, of course.

I got a call from the director Andre Starcevich. He thought I might be in his vampire film. Lev heard Andre came from a family that had been somebodies in Austria-Hungary, politicians, or their advisors, or men of property and influence in that history book empire. Peter heard something similar but placed the family in France, white Russians perhaps? There were names changed, the chatter of industrial fortunes, fascist collaboration or murky deals to get people and money across borders. But Peter and Lev said that was vague gossip with the old men in film. Money always came from somewhere and most often it was accumulated back in a bad situation. Everyone said, they said, Andre was in person a gentleman with private school habits of speech, manners, and tact. A delight to be with at dinners and screenings. He had a wife and child who lived in the Alps, they stayed there while Andre pursued his art, which was in the beginning theater but had then become film.

Because of this whispered safety net of his family, Andre had been able to leap, at a young age and without hesitation, into the theater. His father and older brother, his uncles and grandfathers were sober men of law and business, but he believed in art and because they loved him, the family supported this fool's errand. He'd gotten fired by prestigious theater companies only to appear again, charming and dressed in smooth tweeds.

Andre had mounted shows in London and Paris. His version of *Alice in Wonderland* was an experimental sensation and toured the world. During periods of directing, he apparently acted totally insane. Lev and Peter had heard of physical violence, screaming matches, and things staged in working abattoirs. But they'd also heard about bells chimed and group meditation and trances, extreme feelings of love. The stories about him were split between hellion and family man, but one who left this family to direct religious-tinged endeavors in the Atlas Mountains and the Kashmir region, the island of Zanzibar and Port of Marseille. Andre had a guru. He wanted to make pictures that would transcend divisions between fact and fiction. He'd had cameras broken; film canisters confiscated by military police but had also directed a film set all in one room and taking place in some approximation of real time.

I'd seen Andre's room film at a matinee at the Paris Theater. He'd managed to make it tragic without anything overly sad happening. It was soaked in sorrow like a cake in honey. I wept. But perhaps that was just the state I was in when I saw it. I could not explain where the great emotion came from. It was not in the words, or palette, or even the framing, but in the places where the actors would pause. What they wanted to say, what hovered behind their lines created in me, as a watcher, the feeling of a black pit. As if I could see into a deep cave and feel its hidden, crypt-cool air touching my face. Somehow, watching Andre's film made you aware of a whole other film hidden beneath the one you were watching. And while the one you were actually watching was good and striking, the tension between the story and the unsaid became so unbearable you had to cry.

I went to Andre's hotel suite on a day of heavy snow. As advised by Lev, I dressed to be looked at, for the eye to touch, in pink and lavender silk, with thin layers nestled under a shearling coat. My shiny knee-high leather boots gave a hint of Weimar exchanges, come-hither glances, salty acts in dark doorways.

Andre was wiry. He had the kind of body you'd embrace expecting frailty only to find a density that could hold you tight. Maybe like how a fly feels with a spider. His height and hidden strength made him intimidating. He had a face like a classical musician with rings under his eyes not from illness but from obsession.

He wore an ink-blue fisherman's sweater and a tweed blazer. He liked the cold, he said. I did too. He'd been to California before this and didn't care for it, not the landscape nor the people. Their form of ease seems so lonely and violent underneath. I told him I hadn't been since childhood. Lucky you, he said.

He ordered a pot of hot water, plus milk and sugar. A chambermaid brought it up on a tray. Andre had his own tin of

Lapsang souchong. This was the first time I'd ever heard of or tasted that and I liked it very much. I took one of the foreign cigarettes he offered. The snow fell thick on the other side of the windows. We were doubly inside because the storm had enclosed the city in walls of drifting particles. Falling snow curtains and falling snow walls.

At first, Andre said he wanted us to read a scene together, but we never actually got to it though I stayed for hours. He said, this was not an audition, I already had the part if I wanted. Rather, I might choose to interview him that afternoon. He said I should not be fooled by the supernatural subject matter of the script. The project would not be trash even though it might present itself with a bit of shock and tits.

He wanted to make a war film, a picture of guilt and disgust, self-hatred mixed with the desire to destroy another. But he felt the best way to get there was roundabout, while wearing a disguise. We cannot, will not speak of actual war. Our defenses have gotten so sophisticated that you have to hypnotize people to get them to feel again. Pure image, minimal speaking. We know from horror that an image only glimpsed can be far more terrifying than one seen straight on.

Eyes are vaginas. Images enter with an immediate, sexual intensity if you'll forgive my crudeness. But then, the mind is a womb that gestates and holds and expands. Andre pulled out a folder of pages cut from magazines. He wanted me to read a book called *Story of an Eye*. These are Karl Blossfeldt photographs, he said, as he flipped through images of close-up leaves in black and white, so intricate in detail they seemed both bodily and decorative. He had an image of a street beside a canal made abstract by thick mist. He had another of a woman in high heels with seams up the back of her legs. He flipped the page to a reaper with a scythe, then an illustration of a woman in a ruby dress beside a cornucopia of fruit. Did you know women with TB were thought to be both sexually alluring and terrifying because of their disease, he asked. So pale, eyes large and haunted, lips tinted red with spittle of blood. He sighed.

Andre had so much energy. He showed me a picture of a pile of mummified bodies from a village in Mexico. He'd taken them himself and also shot film footage there he planned to use. Then his elegant musician hands rearranged the pictures to show me a close-up of a flower stem that looked like ironwork. Here then was a woman's face split between light and shadow. Beside that he laid a photo of two legs of a cow that had been sawed off at the knee joint. The legs leaned gracefully against a bare wall. The collage on the coffee table made sense to my nerves though I couldn't follow all the threads of reference.

He said he'd watched me since *Saint Barbara* but what cinched it was a scene of me in *Midnight to Six*. I believed you'd really hurt yourself, you were possessed and hurling yourself against that wall. And yet you survived. Andre asked if I was ready to give my whole self to this strange project. I said yes though I wasn't positive I was actually capable of doing what he asked.

———

God willing, we would shoot in Austria over the summer, Andre said. His producer knew all the details and kept him honest. The fascism up there is still intact, he said, just under the surface of regular life. It hides in papers in the priest's study. It lingers in the police station and cleans up at the butchers after closing. Things haven't changed so much since the war except that now, it is the killers feel persecuted. They aren't though. When the mayor speaks to the retired general, the gas lamps flicker. A terror runs through the wires that hum over the main village street. It's the town my wife comes from, he smirked at this detail, and her family treats me well. But when I chat with certain people, the hairs on the back of my neck quiver.

The hotel ashtray was full. Andre called room service for more hot water. He leaned back on the couch, exhausted. If only talking to investors was as pleasurable as presenting this to you. All the caffeine and ideas ran through my nervous system, making me flicker like a haunted house. All that I'd had that day before coming was grapefruit juice and Dexedrine. When you're starving all sorts of things can ignite the senses. Andre wanted real actors? Was I one? I ended up babbling on about my father and my husband, about training vs. intuition. I fluctuate, I said, between flayed sensitivity and inert lump.

I said I wanted nothing more than to be an instrument for his vision.

He kissed both my cheeks and I took the elevator down to the ground floor. I went out and walked over a carpet of clean white snow.

One morning that winter the phone rang and it was my father's second wife. I'd never heard her voice before. It's Jeanie, she said across the distance. It took some beats before I made sense of what that meant. I told your father I wanted to get in touch. Oh?

They were coming to D.C. for my father's work and wanted to pop up to New York and stay overnight so we could all have dinner. They would be coming in March and wouldn't that be a lovely time in the capital, with the cherry blossoms, magnolia trees, and all? My father must have been coerced by Jeanie, for he was not in the habit of popping in or taking in the spring blooms.

The unknown Jeanie at the other end of the line had a sense of propriety. She had a grown son herself, she said. They'd visited him in California, so it was only fair. She knew what a warm gesture was. My family never normally indulged such things but she was making changes. If they were to fly that far anyhow, how could they not see his flesh and blood? You can't not see your own daughter when we'll be so close. A second wife would say such a thing. We'd get to know one another, Jeanie enthused. So, I replied yes of course, we would be delighted. Lev and I would play a couple who dined with the wife's parents as if it were a normal, natural occurrence.

I got off the phone and retreated to the maid's bath in order to not think more about my father.

While smoking in the bath I thought about my mother. It was her habit of coming to me like that, or it was me setting the conditions that invited her in.

A psychoanalyst I saw for a while asked if my mother didn't sometimes take over my own sense of self. She did of course. I got lost in her memories, her details. I told the doctor I wanted to release myself from the structure of her stories, but I left him before learning how to do that. Dr. Weiss was never going to help me, if I could help it. I just stopped going to see him. He called to say we should meet to discuss me not coming in. Maybe I didn't want my mother to leave, who would I be, after all, without her pain?

She was a knot behind my belly button, a pressure against my spine. My pale body in the bath was the land and above my horizon rose a puff of gray-white smoke into the atmosphere of the air shaft. The smolder started deep within the cave of me.

I emerged from my mother. I was once a pain behind her belly button. She was a grown woman who wept often in front of me and my father, even as she kept hidden the true edge of her tragedy. My mother had a blondness that did a lot of talking for her. A fair child begat a blond woman that was my mother, and she begat a child who was me. At first the silent sound of the color of her hair was what people heard when she opened her mouth, and then, once she killed herself, the blond words were replaced by blood words.

My mother once lived in New York, my city, long before my birth, when she was a child. She'd been young in the din of bad housing overfilled with northern European immigrants who were full of injury and fury. They'd spoken their old language over her head when it was still soft. Her German mother cooked liver with onions and boiled porridge. She brewed watery coffee, not because it's what she wanted but to make the grounds go further. My grandmother made my child mother sit at the table until she finished whatever was served. Sometimes out of stubbornness my mother sat for hours while the bad dish before her grew colder and therefore worse. Without rhyme or reason one day my grandmother trundled my mother out of their apartment and onto a train that took them west where a man willing to marry my grandmother lived. That man would be my mother's destroyer, though nobody knew it at the time.

I got out of the bath. I thought about my young mother and my young father. I left them in the bath under my cloud of steam.

I dressed and went out into a misty day. The park looked hazy because there had been cold rain. Because I'd been crying my vision was blurred. At a diner I sat at the counter under the hanging fixtures of yellow light. I ordered a scoop of cottage cheese. It came served on a leaf of iceberg. I ordered a coffee and stirred in two sugars. I didn't think about my father and Jeanie coming. I didn't think about what I would wear, what I would talk about, or where we would take them for dinner. I needed Lev so badly but he wouldn't be back for weeks.

I took a train downtown to meet Suzanna. She wanted my advice on a gift for her new boyfriend. We stroked shirt fronts and pocket squares, smelled oils from India and soaps from France. But she couldn't decide and we left the store empty-handed. I needed to go back home and we embraced at the portal to the underworld of the subway. Darkness fell at once as happens in winter. I went to bed as soon as I got in. Lev was still a thousand miles away.

Lev returned from Reno sunburned and frustrated by money. He spent long hours on the phone with people in Los Angeles, and also other people in Rome.

Outside, New York spring played around the edges of our consciousness. Lev said the season always changed like this. After a day or two of sun, rain and cold breeze would return. Pigeons sat on the fire escapes getting wet when it rained. They didn't have the will or good sense to seek shelter. When it wasn't raining the males chased the females in lazy mating dance circles.

My father and his second wife came up from D.C.

As a favor to me Lev arranged the dinner for my father and the unknown Jeanie. They arrived via the Amtrak at five o'clock on a Friday. Lev chose Petrucci's, a red sauce place. You could stay a long time in the red leatherette booths or in the wooden chairs arranged around circular tables, ordering as many small dishes as you wanted. You could order drinks from the long bar until you were thoroughly drunk. Behind was a mirror that doubled everything. I had stared into it many nights while Lev joked with his friends. Petrucci's had a familial way of treating diners that still remained respectful and old-fashioned. Each table was decorated with a few carnations in a vase. The owners liked Lev and always brought us free grappa and maybe a slice of cake at the end of the night.

Lev said to my father and Jeanie, he wanted them to have a dinner they couldn't get out west. Jeanie said as long as there wasn't too much garlic in the food, she was easy to please. I knew right away this foolproof choice was wrong.

My father had gotten old. He wore a bolo tie to advertise his Western bona fides and peered at the paper menu quizzically from behind his plastic-rimmed glasses. Jeanie's silver and turquoise, her blouse and cardigan communicated desert country club, churchgoing in the Sunbelt.

After checking with my father and meeting a confused look, Lev took charge, ordering a bottle of Lambrusco, the antipasto supremo, baked clams, and caponata. I felt embarrassed by all of this. I remembered my father's plates of saltines and tuna spiced only with black pepper, his deep distrust of excess, or what some might call flavor. I should have made a reservation at a hotel restaurant, something with nice steaks and pure white potatoes.

Lev uncorked his attention and it bubbled up. He assured the table to speak up if something tickled their fancy. Jeanie asked if we could get at least a green salad, and she, a wine spritzer. They hardly drank back home.

Fearing an awkward silence, I opened up my bag of borrowed anecdotes. Suzanna had seen Lucille Ball attending a Broadway show and I pretended Suzanna was me. Ms. Ball had such a presence, you know? Even just sitting in the audience she attracted one's eye. Jeanie nodded. They didn't watch much television or movies, she kept busy with hiking and crafts.

Had Jeanie heard about the benefits of macrobiotic cooking? I pretended to be a healthier version of myself. They say the way you cut your vegetables changes the health properties. She rolled her eyes. Your father would be fine if everything came from a can. It's such a struggle to get fresh produce up on the hill.

I asked Jeanie about her son and she warmed up. Sipping at her spritz she described Greg's arc from PhD student at UChicago to junior analyst at the Livermore lab. Very prestigious place, she said. Your father could tell you what they do. Those two could talk all day about the work without me understanding, but I'm proud. Too many of Greg's classmates have gone crazy. Kids he grew up with have dropped out of school, are doing drugs. One had moved to Canada and another to Panama. He has a friend who'd been arrested for protesting. There should be room to question the government of course, Jeanie said, but this madness on campuses and on the streets won't do any good.

Lev had got my father going about engineering. It was the easiest path to engagement. Wind him up and watch him spin. Well of course I can't tell you about the classified stuff, or I could but then I'd have to kill you. They laughed at the joke.

The waiter came back burdened, Lev had continued ordering in rounds. Octopus with lemon. Sauce-heavy pasta that threatened Jeanie's pale slacks. The table was heaped with food that we were only picking at. Jeanie ordered another drink. The waiter smiled softly. He had hair curling past his collar, not exactly a hippie but in a style that showed some rebellion.

The problem I was working on back then, my father explained, it's been solved now and anybody can read about it in the journals. But at the time it was vexing. In simple terms it had to do with implosion. The initiator problem was nontrivial. We had to make something that was quiet, really quiet and then suddenly burst, you see? Lev nodded. A neuron gets emitted at a high degree and makes the necessary burst. Well, there are better initiators now but back then this caused us all a lot of trouble. My father had pulled out a pocket notebook and started sketching away. He filled a page with a drawing of a diamond shape with rays, triangles, and dashed lines coming out of it. Dad, I interrupted, Lev doesn't need a lecture. But Lev brushed me off. He promised he was fascinated.

In my drunkenness I said to Jeanie I'd read in the paper that one of the girls at Kent State had had a pet kitten she carried around campus. I said that maybe all these years of the dead children on the television, the glow of burning jungles, the putrid vapors rising out of politicians' mouths, maybe that was what got the young in the streets. Surely that's understandable? I asked. I felt Lev's look from across the table.

Jeanie didn't respond, just excused herself to the ladies' room. My father did not hear. With him, one was unable to tell if he was truly not listening or just skilled at nonengagement. The absent professor is not just a caricature, it's a true state of being for some. Lev waved for the check.

———

My father lived within a concrete bunker of government mythology that I could never puncture. Maybe each of us lives in our own fiction, but it was my father's particular one I always wanted to crack open.

What is propaganda if not theater? My father was audience and player, true believer and wise interpreter all at once. If you offered up a criticism of the US government, he'd say he already knew or that the officials' hands were tied by historic conditions.

Like an actor, my father had an ethical framework made out of imaginary *if*s. What if what had not been, could be? The atom bomb. The hydrogen bomb. What if what has been, had to be? Uranium refined. Atoms split. The scientists had to do it all because it could be done. Nature made it possible and because it was possible it was inevitable.

I aways thought the problems with his *if*s were human in scale. If the bomb was invented, if it was dropped, then it was a triumph of centuries of science. People had harnessed the power of the sun. And if in the process other people—women and kids and men with limps, foolish humans moving about their lives— died at the other end, well it was regrettable but inevitable.

There were weapons that could exist. It was possible the Nazis were working on them. They weren't, but they could have been. And then by the time of European defeat, the US government had spent so much money. If the US had not made them then the Nazis would have. That was the story. Only the Nazis didn't have a real program and we, the government, didn't use what was created on the Nazis, a fact elided in the narrative. The story goes if we hadn't dropped the bomb on Japan tens of thousands of Americans would have died in the land invasion. And if the second bomb hadn't been dropped on Nagasaki, the emperor would not have been shaken enough to surrender. If. Then. If the US had not built up a sufficiently compelling military and cultural sphere of influence then communism would spread. And then?

Power teeters but ultimately finds equilibrium with the aid of dedicated custodians. America had emerged from the war burdened with the task of leading the free world. That's what the story said. We were now fated to live under the sword of Damocles, my father thought. Once the bomb is thought it is real. My father believed in scientific mastery. The physical world had rules beyond us and our job was to learn them. Then we could be happy. Peace could come through strength. If people could calm down, we could progress. We could move toward a better tomorrow if only people could behave. My father didn't consider himself an ideologue. Rather he saw himself as a man of science operating under the pressures and special conditions of his time.

In the old days, people used to torture one another in the public square. Death was meted out with stones, horses, and bonfires lit beneath living bodies. Or there were wars in which people slogged in the mud, got gangrene and dysentery, and fought for years on end. Was this better, my father would ask. That, he said, was barbarity.

Here, now, nothing more than a few flips through the chapters of a history book, men had brought us into the bright and terrifying future.

Liberty is good but not everyone is ready.

My father wasn't a cruel man. He had his good points and his weaknesses. He was quite sensitive, with a mental antenna turned toward invisible emanations. He used to say how beautiful his problems were. He'd tried to show me as a child, speed and velocity, weight as it differs from density. Nothing, he said, works as you assume it might. Everything is made of complex configurations. Atoms consist of smaller particles, electrons and protons and neutrons, held together somehow but with space between. I never learned.

It's beautiful, he used to say, but I could not see.

I'm not a scientist, I'm an actress. That is the easiest identity to dismiss. How could I attack the great power he belonged to?

I suspect my father didn't actually think of me that often and when he did it was with a vague, melancholic affection. You were such a thoughtful little girl. Of my films he always said he supported them, as long as I was happy.

One fine day the small cast of Andre's vampire picture arrived at a property on the outskirts of Döllersheim, Austria. The village itself had a handful of businesses: a grocery and tavern, a gas station and a butcher, and a stationery store where they had mail service, coffee, and schnapps. The buildings were all arranged along a strip of road with steep hills climbing up behind. We were up high with a panoramic view of the forests that grew in the valley below.

The real inhabitants of the village ignored us the few times we showed our faces. We were not worth their attention. The men of the region worked mostly for the state forestry department, or at the paper mill farther down the mountain. They drove compact trucks painted red or pine green, or else they rode on shiny black, well-maintained motorcycles. The motorcycles belonged to the bachelors and the trucks to the fathers. Young or old they dressed in coveralls. The men talked in huddles outside the tavern. The mothers wore no-nonsense dresses while the young girls wore miniskirts. The women walked everywhere unless they had their arms wrapped around the waist of one of the men on their motorbikes, and only the young girls did that. These people lived in another movie parallel to ours. Theirs was one of austere rusticism.

We hardly went into town, except on excursions to send letters or to buy cigarettes and wine. We lived for the time of our shoot as temporary folk of an imaginary place called cinema. It was close to Döllersheim, but you could only enter through a portal invisible to the untrained eye.

Our time unfolded in the hidden world, at a disused estate, surrounded by green meadows and below distant, snow-dusted, blue-gray peaks that were so pristine they appeared as if they'd been painted by MGM artists back when color was new. Bells clinked from the necks of cows and you could hear them at a great distance.

Andre and his wife had secured this place for our group preparations, which he promised would be arduous. He said it was essential we develop trust and rapport. We would need to create a temporary community for the success of the film. Put aside your scripts he said, you already have the words. You do not yet have yourselves or the feel of one another. Let go of what is given and begin the work of spirit.

We listened to records of traditional songs recorded by traveling scholars and sung and played by old people who remembered. Andre's wife woke us before dawn for calisthenics and breath exercises she'd learned from her guru. She led us through dances that went in circles until the moon came out. We chanted lines of dialogue and practiced scenes under hypnosis. We sat with our knees touching in a sauna that had once been a bunker, sweating and holding hands. Andre said all this work was to dissolve some of our old habits and bring us to a higher vibration.

I came to doubt all my boundaries. One night after our rounds of dancing I was able to jump onto the top of a six-foot-tall stone wall without difficulty. My skin was cool to the touch. When I caught sight of my reflection in an upper-story window I thought yes, she is a spirit, she is undead. Perhaps it was the altitude. I do not mean that I lost my boundaries in an abstract way. Physically I could not tell where I ended and the landscape began.

It was hard to think of life down below. I'd call Lev but then find myself mute with too much experience. He was distracted by his own things. In my absence Lev's son was living at home over the summer. They were talking theory and Lev wanted to include me. He'd ask me a question like, do you think you struggle for some positive version of freedom, or only against restriction? Do you have a conception of freedom for, or only freedom from? Then before I could think of an answer, he would start describing the bold actions taken by some guerillas in South America. He had a lot to say about these bloodthirsty politicians sending men to massacre and die. Had I been reading the news? I had not.

I'd be falling asleep on the other end of the line. I have an idea for a film and I want to shoot it fast. You'll be in it. Now he said, was the time to mix our reality with our fictions. But we had many time zones and moods to overcome, I thought. Our ties were frayed. I'd say I needed to go to bed, we'd hang up and I'd lose consciousness.

All our preparatory intensity with Andre came to its culmination in a two-day period right before we were to begin shooting. Andre said we were to travel through a membrane and come out in the time of our story. Now will be then. That morning, he led us to an empty barn. As if we were his children he said, I am so proud of the hard work you've done. What comes next will be hard, and you may hate me, he said, but no matter how uncomfortable it is, you must not leave the barn. If you leave the room, you will be leaving the film altogether. He said if we didn't stay together our art would ring false and any artificiality would be a disgrace to the story we were here to tell. Our story is make-believe but the horror must be honest.

We could drink what Andre and his assistant provided but there would be nothing to eat. We had had nothing to eat the day before. Though he did not tell us then, I knew after that what we were given to drink was infused with something psychoactive.

We spent hours crawling in the dark, cavernous space. The floor was earth mixed with hay that had been packed down a long time before. Nothing smelled like cows anymore because the animals had long ago gone. The darkness smelled like pine tar. The room had been warmed by the long day and was now cooling around us.

During our slow circuits we encountered one another. We felt one another's shoulder or foot, cheek or calf when we bumped together. Andre had instructed us to touch in greeting and then move on without speaking whenever we found each other. We weren't supposed to linger. But there were moments of caresses and even a kiss in those first hours.

The periods of quiet shuffling, breath, and sounds from the environment outside were broken up by Andre's voice every so often. He spoke from different parts of the room with new instructions and images. His voice, now hoarse, now bell clear, served as our beacon.

After many hours the lights blazed on. We saw one another disheveled and sweaty on the floor. We drank more tea before he sent us back under.

Remember, he said. That was our exercise under surveillance, under a veil of artificial dark and real night. He kept prompting us to remember. I projected myself back. My trance had phases like the moon.

I remembered. I pictured.

My absent-minded father stood in a circle of electric light, haloed by moths. He has always been a man with the highest of security clearances. An anointed priest of electrical engineering, physics, and explosives. Out beyond him in the desert were coyotes in the tall grasses, bald tires on their sides, barbed-wire fences. He walked back into our house where secrecy preceded him across our Navajo rug. The secrecy disrobed and crawled across my bed and then into my parents' room, shutting the door behind. In the circle of light where my father had been, a plume of dust rose and then settled.

I remembered myself as I had been years earlier, in the city with my body at its extreme of thinness. I did not eat. I slept with anyone while being cute and sweet. I wore sheer stockings with heels. I left them on even as I stripped off everything else. I had the hustle and bustle that was refreshing. Then I had a big break, as they call it.

There before me were all the other women I had been over the years. I looked at them first one way and then another. They were many and singular, as a person is when reflected in two facing dressing room mirrors. They had taken so many streets to end up here with me. In the city they had been boozy, busty, sweaty, and hardworking under harsh lights. Then with twists, social climbs, hair brushed perfectly smooth, they had remade themselves into one girl. Her bare legs were smooth. She strolled around a lovely village in a minidress.

It had taken so much training to make my face a mask that could cover them all. I saw myself, one of my selves, walking down the dirt road alone, leaving a vacation house in tears, a hysterical woman wearing only a bikini and a borrowed shirt. It would be her own fault if she died by some silly accident or by the hand of some man driving by who decided pull over.

To be a playful girl took nerves of steel. Thread-fine steel like tempered piano wire wrapped around the neck. That's what it felt like even though I know very well nerves run up and down our bodies, not around and around.

I started singing in the dark, laughing to myself at the whole picture. I could remove her from my body, like a seed from its cherry, red and slippery. If I wanted, I could remove her from myself.

As Andre said, acting is not dishonesty. Acting has nothing to do with artifice. Rather, to do it well is to make a demonic arrangement with yourself. You walk along the edge of deep craters and across mist-blanketed valleys. You see other versions of yourself and your character as desiccated husks. Acting is a narrow path.

Along your journey you meet others who've made the same bargain as you. They might be religious pilgrims or bandits wandering the desolate lands as the wind whistles. You play out scenes together and part ways.

We are not born equal in this reality Andre said. We are free only in some striving, desperate sense. Because we are here, tasked and gifted with time to act, we must feel simply everything. As if our skins have been removed.

You trade in pieces of yourself, lumps of flesh with fat on top, to keep going. Your body is all you have of value. You make exchanges to gain access to the consciousness of others. To enter them and draw awareness from them. It's wrong perhaps but you cannot stop. This is a dangerous journey. You are not supposed to go that way but you would trade anything for the feeling you get, you would walk your feet raw.

The camera is like a bomb. It is like the core where the chain reaction occurs but it is also like the blast flash. No one is meant to have too much exposure. It can be lethal. The camera penetrates not only people but the material of the world. Trees, houses, people walking across a bridge, and the bridge itself. The camera's light catches even those far-off horses that were, only a moment before, grazing peacefully in their field. The light penetrates through the skin but also caresses the surface. A blinding light flashed through the window. I flung my arm over my eyes.

I could not stop remembering. Even occurrences I had not experienced directly came to me while I was enthralled by Andre's vampire picture.

I remembered that once, when blackout drunk, my mother's stepfather Raymond set their house on fire. They were living in California at the time. She was a girl.

He was smoking in bed and an ember caught a blanket that lit the lampshade, which ignited a curtain. The room was small and papered, draped thickly and furnished with cheap wooden items. My grandmother, a young woman, smelled smoke from the other room. In a room aflame she shook him while my mother watched in a trance. Call emergency like I taught you, my grandmother yelled, take your brother outside. The stepfather stayed unconscious through smoke and siren wails and even when a mess of men with axes and buckets barged in. A young fireman heaved him out, over-the-shoulder-style, like his body was a sack. But even after they'd dragged him out and sprayed the walls into charred submission, he stayed unconscious. It was as if he were dead.

Light from the firetruck and police car illuminated the outside face of the rental house in circling flashes. The lights only reached the leaf tips of the orange grove trees across the street. Usually my mother could smell them, but that night the burnt smell won out. In the aftermath, the mattress was pulled out onto the lawn. Where the stepfather's body had lain was pink and wrinkled sheet cloth. All around, outlining his shape, it was burned black.

Raymond came through unharmed except for the loss of his eyebrows and lashes. No one explained how. Like when someone gets in a crash while drunk and climbs out unharmed after killing everyone in the other car. His body went limp. His body did not burn. He didn't die and made it even a funny story he told down at the legion hall. He had many such anecdotes. There was the one about being thrown from a truck on a logging road, and the time he was almost run through the gut with a metal rod while working in a military garage in Saint-Nazaire, France. Where the naked ladies dance, he would say whenever someone said the word "France." He couldn't help himself. He laughed as he recounted fights and blackouts and bone-breaking incidents.

My grandmother pursed her mouth tight, then took a sip of her drink. She worked extra hard to shape herself into what Ray wanted, Kewpie doll eyes, red bow lips, a swish of golden hair. They'd met dancing. At the beginning, he'd been her savior. Girls who had babies out of wedlock could not be too choosy, she'd thought. But then he came along with big offers, muscled arms, and native-born American know-how, and she though, how lucky am I?

In Sacramento, when my grandmother was pregnant with the uncle I never knew, Ray pushed her down some stairs. My mother cried as she struggled to help her mother up. It's all right dear, it was an accident. Can you get me a glass of water? The next home my grandmother found for them had only one story. That would solve things. That old song and dance. The next blowout Ray choked her against a wall and well, every house has to have those, don't they? He broke the rod on which the clothes hung then disappeared in a rage, came back home two days later with a dozen roses and a heart charm on a chain, begging forgiveness. She said, it's okay honey, but it never was. She painted the kitchen a magazine popular shade of peach, to cheer things up a bit. In that room she chain-smoked and drank cup after cup of weak coffee. She kept slim and well-groomed even as she grew more and more furious with the way things were.

My mother's half brother was born with a club foot that needed mending and that cost something. Ray said it was money that got him mixed up. He worked as an insurance adjuster and had first-rate penmanship and an eye for paperwork slipups. He had some college, but not enough.

At Christmastime he and his colleagues exchanged bottles of liquor for jobs well done and whatever was in the bottles flowed into Ray. Even all the years later when I was a child, my mother got the most depressed during the holidays.

My mother went to school and her teachers were nuns who drilled the girls in geometry and the lives of saints. After school she stayed at home to watch the baby while my grandmother worked. My mother found a bit of calm in watercolors and pencils and a pad. Time disappeared into paintings she made of still lifes of roses and scarves and pieces of wood she arranged on the table in the peach kitchen. Years passed like this in a fugue.

I remember these things even though I was not alive. The damage was done. The damage was done in rented places and in a house with a peach kitchen that burned but where they continued to live after the fact.

Raymond interfered with my mother. That was Aunt Karla's turn of phrase. Maybe that's why she took her own life, Karla said. Ray took her life maybe, I thought.

All my life when mother was alive she stuttered that she was hurt. She was hurt and the man who did the damage said he could not remember. If my grandmother confronted him, I don't know. Ray never meant to hurt anyone. That's what he said when he cried. She took him back time after time because what could she do, after all women couldn't even have their own bank accounts and she had two children, the first out of wedlock. My grandmother got distracted and let her daughter float. She worried about the future and could not hold her golden-haired daughter in her gaze in the present. The California glare, and the drinks, and depression were too much. On top of all that, maybe she had a head injury.

Raymond had no memory. My grandmother was confused. My mother forgot then remembered then told the women who would listen. He died of drink, my grandmother of heart failure. My mother's half brother died in a car accident when I was two. When my mother was a girl she died repeatedly under the weight of her stepfather. Step, falter, step down again with full force.

My mother thought that what was right was when adults protected the young. She thought to herself that was justice. But her ancestors lived in the old world and her mother didn't have what you call options. What's more to the point is that my mother learned that in the Western tradition many children are sacrificed. She was, not once but repeatedly. And since the man was blackout drunk and could not remember he had to do it again and again. Nights fell. It went without saying, without being mentioned.

Once a child is marked by the scars of sacrifice others in the community pull back. They lose their sight. The child becomes a phantom. A person can be a phantom while studying, working, even marrying. They are most often recognized as what they are by other phantoms, which does the society little good. A phantom can give birth to a living child. A phantom can read the writing on the wall and so can I. I remembered this for my family while in the dark of the barn.

Andre's film begins with a prologue, a montage of real bodies preserved by the arid conditions of their catacombs.

Unlike the Egyptian kind, these mummies were not wrapped in cloth. They were hunched or curled up like babies in the womb. The leather of their skin stretched over their white skulls with mouths open in silent screams. Shawls and bits of clothing flutter around these faces frozen in extremis, more threads than fabric in the high contrast cinema light.

Unlike the Egyptians, these Mexican villagers had never intended to transform their loved ones so. The dead had been interned during a cholera epidemic, so the bodies had been hidden away by the living immediately after death arrived. The salty air had mummified them naturally. Officials, so desperate to prevent the spread of the disease, and overcome by the sick, even entombed a few while they still lived. Some, Andre told us, were buried alive. The officials learned this later when they found one body facing down, stuck in a pose with her teeth around her own arm and her mouth full of petrified blood.

These bodies are strange in the way reality is also. Stretched and small in a way no prop maker could sculpt. You wouldn't learn any of this just watching the film. I only learned about the origins of the material from speaking to Andre directly. The prologue is pure horror, but their desiccated remains weigh down what fiction you see next even though they look on the verge of crumbling to dust.

After that opening Andre flies the audience on bat wings up to the cold, old Alps. We have journeyed to a time before death camps and telephones. The fields are not the light green of spring budding but the decaying gold of fall harvest, of coming night. We see waterfalls and mountain passes, wooden houses lodged in dim valley shadow and sublime white light raying outward from behind up-jutting peaks. This is the land of ancient black alder, curls of smoke, glinting eyes of animals, dense nothing. Virtuous maids and suspicious farm wives who turn their kerchiefed heads away from travelers. I cannot say how Andre communicated all this, for it was not what was in the frame exactly, but more in the music and the slowness of the camera. What we do see is women in big skirts working in a humid field. They bend over deep; their torsos and heads and arms disappear. They appear to have been cut in half at the waist, so it looks like there are only soft behinds in billowing skirts out there in the field.

Then we come to the village where interiors hide themselves behind shutters that close shyly behind flower boxes. Andre shows a tower with doors that open once an hour and expel wooden figures that spin mechanically for a moment before they're pulled back by the workings of the clock.

Ages pass. Carts pulling hay roll down a rutted dirt path.

A new section of the film starts in another place. It is a large city, we are led to believe, with canals and tidy bright buildings facing them to make reflections. There are the pastel buildings made of plaster and then just below them, reflected in the black smooth of the waterways are their wavering twins.

In one of these buildings a junior agent is told by an old man he must travel to the Transylvanian village to finalize the purchase of an estate.

I was this junior agent's wife. He comes home to me and showers me in kisses. I am in a dress with lace and a large soft collar. I beg him not to go. I have been plagued in the days before his departure by horrible premonitions and nightmares. I see what is coming. He assures me all would be well and that the funds he will earn will help us start our life properly.

As my character, my face was haloed by a black mass of hair. The makeup woman made me paler as the time of the movie progressed so that by the end, I was marble white. My mouth was red and my kohled eyes perpetually wide. Andre, she, and I conspired on how I would look, that is already dead, yet glowing like a tubercular wraith. I hid within a fur-lined cape. I hurried along an oil-dark canal.

Johann departs. He travels many weeks over sea then land to meet the reclusive buyer. He stops at an inn for the night. He is quite close now, his destination hides further up in the mountains, within a dense fog.

Andre shows us glinting of animal eyes hidden within a larch that shivers in the wind.

The scene moves to the interior of a village inn. Around a table, farmers and woodsmen whisper of skinned sheep and sucked bones, gas smells and fainting daughters. To Johann the innkeeper and the gypsy women say, don't go. Though he hears, he remains fixed on his task. Johann is supernaturally compelled toward the castle.

The townsmen continue drinking and talking low about people disappearing, their corpses turning up later broken and drained. Everyone knew that plants grew best where the most blood had been spilt. Their valley had been especially verdant this year. Best not ask why. In the high pastures the rampion had grown vivid purple and all the expecting mothers craved some.

The next morning Johann awakes from a powerful dream. He sees the castle that is his aim appear for a moment before it is swallowed again in the mist. In the rocks there is a chasm with a narrow road that runs alongside a fast-flowing stream, but Johann needs a means of travel.

No such castle exists, says a coachman. You are mistaken. Please, says Johann. I must appear. I am expected. I haven't any horses, says the coachman as he brushes with long firm strokes a smoke-black horse.

Johann is too much a coward to say what needs to be said. He does not have the words.

White cows cluster in an emerald field below a gray peak. Johann decides to walk the rest of the way beside the flowing stream, and under the waterfall's overhang with its moss and slippery, echoing enclosure. The coachman with a coach pulled by four white horses gallops past.

Ignoring the pleas and warnings he has heard at every turn, Johann goes. Spurred on by the mystery and the desire to know even at the cost of his life, Johann goes, ascending on foot. In his mental simplicity, in his will toward death, he ascends the mountain as coal-black night falls from above.

The vampire, cloaked in his feverish plagues, rises to greet him. Then the horrors begin in earnest.

When Andre's shoot was over I was driven down from the village all the way to the Linz Airport. The driver was silent and sturdy and his Mercedes was just as quiet and solid. We hurtled through black green pine forest on a two-lane road. The car was safe, engineered by Germans, so we could travel at this high silver speed. The sky above was the color of a baby blanket.

At the airport I chain-smoked while I waited to depart. I held my passport and a ticket to meet Lev in Athens. I thought about how Lev probably expected me to arrive beautiful. I knew I had become a gaunt monster in the mountains. My gums had turned pale and bloodless and they pulled up so that my teeth looked sharper. All my sexuality had condensed into a single artistic shaft, it glowed up my backbone and made the top of my head tingle. I felt truly old, ancient.

I wondered about how you might make a whole film with scenes that swung open like doors. The audience would pass through one scenario to the next and all that would connect each was one element. I thought about doors and frames and hinges.

Maybe, I thought, there could be a series of actresses all playing the same character. She would change from scene to scene but the film itself would never acknowledge transformations. She could travel far and meet many people. What, I wondered, would be the thread that made the many unite as one?

From the speakers in the airport ceiling a disembodied voice called out first in German and then again in other tongues. Flight Olympic Airways flight 166 for Athens, now boarding.

The same day but in a different reality. Lev was there to kiss me on both cheeks on the other side of customs. He had a car rented and a plan drawn up. We had no time to lose.

Lev was all jet-lag delirium. He'd hurt his back in New York and had been taking pills for the pain. He needed me to take the wheel for a while so he could rest. He knew I hated driving here but it would be just for a few hours, he promised. So, I was once again a foreigner passing through my husband's ancient land, honking and inching and gunning it on hills so the car didn't stall out when we finally got out of the city's orbit and could make up some time.

I was a strange woman hugging cliff roads with a car she couldn't drive so well.

I rolled down the window and the air streamed through. It had sprinkled rain for a moment and the moisture released all the oils both man-made and organic into the air. The buffeting car breezes outside smelled of asphalt and exhaust, it smelled of sappy trees well heated by the sun. The soft brown soil and rows of trees blurred into a binary pattern as I sped us along. Low white buildings appeared before then disappeared behind us; horses and donkeys, mongrels strutting leisurely along, close enough to the cars to make me nervous. A cow lay beneath a lonely tree right beside two kids kicking a soccer ball back and forth. I lit a fresh cigarette.

After a time half asleep with his mouth open, Lev roused himself. He flipped through stations until he found something he liked. He sang along. He touched the back of my neck. Just like that, the vampiric angst began losing its grip. Rapid travel can do that, wipe away one reality and put in its place another. All around the earth different temperatures are happening simultaneously. Cold up high and hot down below. Summer somewhere when it's winter elsewhere. And now with technology one can speed from one reality to the next in a blink. It's too much.

The car quivered as we changed lanes. Our bodies hovered, strapped to the leather seats that were suspended within the metal frame. We hurtled. We sped. The asphalt shimmered black with heat mirages that rose a few feet above the road. A truck overtook us and blew its horn so that I jumped. Speed up for God's sake, that man is going to kill us. We could hurtle into oblivion at any turn. Each new vista could be our last. The wine dark sea rippled mythically at the bottom of the cliffs.

You've got to drive tougher, Lev instructed. I'm just being honest, darling, he said after his next wincing correction, and my angry glance.

As if honesty were a virtue above all else. As if it didn't relate to the power in our marriage. People rarely wave the flag of honesty when they're saying something sweet. He'd wanted me to drive because his head throbbed, but my driving was making it worse. Or something like that. The air between us prickled.

One thing about fights with ones you love is how vivid the details are in the moment and how quickly they blur into a feeling. The criticism wasn't important, but the tone burned my cheeks. Only he and I felt what passed between us in the car and neither of us could have explained it. It wasn't important.

But then he stroked my arm and said, baby. I know you're tired too. I'm sorry. And I was overtaken afresh by Lev.

We stopped at the next town with a gas station. Lev phoned Peter to report our progress. I was once again the American wife smiling vaguely while her husband engaged the proprietor behind the counter in discussions of the heat, the best place to get some fruit for the trip. The man knew Lev wasn't local but Lev made a joke and he laughed and that was more than enough.

I drank a Coke, holding the dew-covered glass to my forehead between sips. Returning to the car Lev said he wanted to drive. Of course. I didn't even want to do it in the first place. You did a good job, sweetheart, all things considered. He rubbed the bridge of his nose in a way that melted me. He had the profile of a saint. I don't even know why I was angry, really.

We leaned side by side on the hood of the car to study the map. The engine underneath our booklet was still making plinking noises of effort from the workout I'd put it through. Lev stuck his finger onto a point in the creased Automobile Touring Club of Greece. According to everyone our destination was not so far.

We got back in and resumed our flight across the asphalt. Billows of cloud gathered above the mountains. It reminded me of the west. Everything stood near still but the silvery cars on this strip of asphalt. The year was nineteen-something. The year just was.

Peter's house was like a sanctuary on a distant planet. Its dome nestled on a hilltop with a steep downward path to a beach. Peter led us around on a tour first thing. He was proud but also disappointed. They were going to sell the place as part of the divorce.

The architect, who was a friend of his, had designed it using modern building techniques but with the aim of conjuring ancient places. The architect belonged to a moment that wanted to build into and with the environment. From the outside the dome curved like a giant helmet pierced with windows for air flow. A few pines, twisted by consistent wind, grew close by, making it seem as if the structure had been there longer than it had. Peter said they'd built it by pouring concrete over a huge balloon. It was a mystical industrial creation.

The walls were thick and rough to the touch. The windows were stained and sent gold and red shapes onto the facing sides of the dome. Peter talked about buildings made to track stars, and ones that stayed cool in the heat and warm during winter nights using nothing but the science of their materials. He threw us references as we followed him around the laurel and bay trees, the carob and figs. Dogon houses, he said. Kivas like in the land you're from, he said. All I could think of was alien planets, the exotic dwellings in science fiction movies.

When he led us inside though, we found furnishings out of step with the structure. There was a TV on a crate and some sun-bleached directors' chairs. The rooms called out for cosmic beauty, but Peter had lost many belongings and much of his joy in his cross-continent divorce. He did and didn't want to talk about Olivia. Her absence hung like a funeral perfume in the house.

As Lev showered, I described the vampire picture to Peter. I told how Andre shot our eyes up close, composed shots of reflections over shoulders so that multiple images came together in single shots. We walked beside a wall of raw crystal. I screamed and screamed for a whole day.

Andre had a way of creating a black hole inside you, I said. Peter nodded.

Again and again, I want to get lost in some piece of art. The process of making a film feels like the only thing that makes living worthwhile, but it's also the thing that takes me away. I put myself in these situations of artificial intensity, with strangers, just to mirror life back to itself. I worry I will lose sight of what's worth living without this kind of pressure.

The next night Peter took us down to a village restaurant that served the best fish and wine. We had a view of the port that was all white gray and lavender blue. I heard a British laugh in the dark but otherwise local voices echoed. Peter knew some men passing the evening with tavli on a leather board. They made friendly remarks. We ate and drank.

I haven't yet told you the story of my brush with death, Peter said. Lev has heard a bit, but not the whole thing. Somehow, I think you'll enjoy my tale of woe.

Olivia and I had been fighting, as we always did. She'd been talking about her brother, her father, and it sent me into a rage, but it was nothing I wasn't already familiar with. I felt possessed by anger all last year. I know now each little thing she said was usual, frustrating sure, but nothing to fly off the handle about. But then I couldn't calm down. You know when you remember the feeling of the fight but not the logic? Or the logic collapses over time and all you're left with is the anger? The strangest incident can tear things apart.

I left the house. I walked a long way and then, on a whim, decided to go for a dip. It was late in the day, but I thought why not, the waters at its warmest even if the air's cool. So, I swim and swim. Closer in to the rocks, some teenagers were fooling around and I went out into deeper water to get away from their antics. For a while I was wrapped up in my grievances, but it's hard to stay angry in the sea. I floated and I thought as I swam out and out.

Before I knew what was happening, a small boat with a motor passed right by me. I must not have been visible. I felt this shock. A blade had caught me but at first, I didn't feel any pain. I didn't even realize. I thought to myself, what a close call, Peter said.

Thank God, a man on the boat saw right away what had happened. He began shouting. Then the teenagers on the shore noticed the commotion. I was moving my arms around, they were fine. I was keeping my head above water in the wake, but then I reached down to my leg and my hand went right in, into a slice. Half my thigh was floated flat like a manta ray, a plume of blood emerging from the cut. Still, I didn't feel a thing.

The boaters understood what Peter didn't. They circled round, saved his life by dragging him up and tourniqueting his leg. They got him to shore and someone ran for a doctor.

Olivia and Peter were on the verge of their divorce then. They had no children. He said everything had come apart quickly, even though they'd had many years together. She has returned to Verona, to stay with her parents. They were monarchists, Peter said, who still had a portrait of Mussolini hanging in a place of honor. I couldn't believe it when I saw it.

He laughed and said that that motor blade had probably kept them together for an extra three months. He'd been so close to death; she couldn't leave until he could walk. Her mothering instincts overwhelmed her hatred.

Lev said he loved the story; it could be a film. Lev would take anything that wasn't bolted down. Please, Peter entreated, let my humiliations remain my own.

Small white boats glimmered and bobbed in the now-blue-black harbor. Each was lassoed to a post. Footsteps sounded on distant stone steps. Everything was spotless and exhausted. We leaned back in our seats. The radio sang to all who were left to hear a ballad of knights in white satin.

I had been asleep on a blanket on the beach, I have no idea for how long, when I heard Peter calling me to consciousness. My cheek was hot from being pressed into worn cotton. The sand beneath had cupped to hold my face. I saw him waving for me at the top of the hill. I climbed the many steps back up to the house. There was a long-distance call for me, Peter said.

Lev had carried the telephone outside onto the patio and set it on the table under the big red-and-white umbrella. The umbrella fluttered, as did Lev's magazines. On one cover was a drawing of a woman walking a tightrope beside the title of the lead article, "Can You Trust Your Own Perceptions?" The magazine was kept from blowing away in the dry wind by the weight of a glass pitcher.

Lev was nodding on the line. All right, he said, I understand. She's here now. Here she is. I'm so sorry. His voice was unreadable to me. He just handed me the phone and went inside. To give privacy I guess.

Hello, the voice on the line said, it's Jeanie. Jeanie of Los Alamos. Jeanie and my father, I thought. Yes. I recognize this voice.

You don't know the trouble I had to go through to find this number, she said, her frustration audible. I wondered, still catching up, what all the fuss was about? I pictured Jeanie wearing some kind of tennis outfit because that's how her voice sounded to me.

Your father had been feeling poorly, she said. He'd gone to the doctor a few weeks earlier and was told he had a mild flu. He was shaky and tired. He'd been napping in the afternoons, which Jeanie said he never did normally.

I hummed with concern, waiting for the point. A few nights ago, Jeanie had woken to him groaning in pain. She called the ambulance and they took him away.

Your father died, Jeanie said.

My heart lies still some days. I cannot feel it even though I know it must be there, beating away inside under the skin. I look down at myself, pull my belly button toward my spine, creating a sucked-in space. I hold until my lungs start to feel panicked, releasing so my belly goes soft and curved at my panty line. I think I should stop drinking and smoking to save my figure and my heart. We all know it's bad and yet it's so relaxing in the moment to get drunk, to laugh and sigh. I put ylang-ylang oil on my inner thighs and vanilla behind the ears. I slap my skin lightly starting at the feet and working my way up. What's good for the circulation is good for the complexion. I read that somewhere. I stand up straight.

Meaningful time, that's what's been destroyed, hasn't it? The myth of time flowing, the feeling that we were bobbing along naturally from birth toward death, it changed this century. I'm no historian but that's how it feels. It feels like now we're all just particles bouncing dumbly around until we get winked out of existence.

I tell Jake one of my stories while we lie in the sagging brass bed. My mother died and then my father died and I lived between them. Now it's now. The story takes hardly any time at all. Except I was young at the beginning and now I'm not.

Films take so long to make and yet watching the finished product takes barely any time at all. A film can cover an hour or an epoch. Two people look at one another across a room. They realize, and the audience sees, they no longer love one another. You can see that break in their eyes, in the close-ups. You can feel it from the music. Watching from the dark auditorium, you start to cry.

It's too much to be sleepy under a CinemaScope sun and receive news of distant death, whispered to you through a crackling line. It is too much but modern life makes it not just possible, but commonplace. The movie camera, the airplane, the bomb, they don't use time right. They make us phantoms, shadows, heaps of particles. I can't bear it.

I traveled on three planes. Rising up and descending, making a waveform across the globe, moving west. Each takeoff was fast enough to pin me back in my seat. The jets accelerated on the runways before pulling their noses up toward the heavens. Stewardesses picked their way down the carpeted path offering meals on a schedule that did not match the dark and light outside. The cabins smelled like baked ham and lamb chops. They offered more wine or an after-dinner drink of Galliano or Old Grand Dad. For dessert, they had a fruit plate or chocolate mousse. These women with their navy neck scarves had so much to offer. I said yes to a brown liquor and used it to wash down my pills. I had no more tears. I swooned back into the firm blue seat.

As soon as I had fallen asleep, the ladies of the sky were back with toast and jam, coffee or tea. It was still early in the morning but there was so much more space to cross. John F. Kennedy Airport. What was the purpose of your journey? Work and also pleasure. The pleasure of working and another flight to catch. Ma'am, what was the primary purpose of your trip?

Aloft again, I dozed and woke. Hollywood was before us, a great mountain chain beneath us. Clouds, eddies of air, I found myself a loose particle rushed along. The plane rattled as our pilot navigated turbulence. The stewardess reminded us to keep our seat belts fastened. I gripped the seat's arm. I quaked.

Beside me was a man my father's age. He looked on with pity. He had a camera slung around his neck and was snapping away out the window. He'd been in Korea, he said, assigned to work in an open-doored helicopter as people down below shot and screamed and died. Nothing since then has scared me much, he said.

Out the plane window the Rockies rose into peaks and fell into canyons and crevices. Deep old tunnels and new industrial blasts marked up earth. Gold and lead, copper and zinc had been extracted from this land. In clear moments you could see evidence by way of strange bright stains that spilled down mountain sides. Whole chunks of landscape were not where they should be. That's where the Donner party died, my seatmate pointed down. He'd read a book all about it.

The air calmed down and he flagged the stewardess for whiskeys before our landing. Would you like one, he offered. Yes, I said, of course.

Attached to the ceiling of my father's garage were two strings with tennis balls hanging at the end. They dangled precisely at the windshield height of his and Jeanne's cars, so that they knew just where to stop to give room to walk between bumper and wall. The tennis balls were the first things that greeted you when your car pulled in. The ball gently thunked. When you opened the door you were greeted by the smell of motor oil and other smells of the practical, mechanical but clean interior.

There were many such details my father had built into this home. My father's eye was trained toward efficiency, quiet, and reason. His big beige Suburban was meant to be parked four feet from the wall, the ball on the string ensured it was.

All my father's tools hung on a pegboard that he'd painted with their shapes in light yellow to indicate where each implement belonged. The handsaw had a hook on the far left above the worktable. The clamps, in ascending size, was meant to be on the right side. A place for everything and everything in its place.

I had never visited this house, never lived here. Yet it was familiar. Each detail was an extension of my father's thinking and his handiwork. The construction had taken him a long time because he did it mostly by himself in the hours after work. He'd first drawn up the blueprints with my mother, me, and perhaps some dreamed-of younger siblings in mind, brothers and sisters who never came to be. My father had been in the process of building it when my mother died. He didn't change the design, only slowed down. When he'd met Jeanie and Greg, they had fulfilled the home's intended purpose.

In their casual living room were two leather-strap armchairs flanking an olive-green wool couch. It was scratchy if you sat on it bare legged. I was the only one who did such a thing though, so it was no one's issue except mine. In this room they'd watch news of the world unspool in a ribbon. Negotiation and conferences, bombing raids and protests and strikes, politicians' fabrications. They had listened there to Walter Cronkite's measured voice as he predicted that Vietnam would end in stalemate. How must my father have felt, watching one war after the next, while still believing the next technological development might be the one to bring a solution?

Jeanie explained with apologies that the spare rooms were occupied by her son and her sister who'd come from Sacramento to help. I would sleep in my father's basement office. It had a couch she'd made up. There were two ways you could get there, out the backdoor and along the porch, or down a built-in ladder that hid behind a door beside the linen closet. I went out the back way.

My father's office had a wide desk and a narrow couch. Though he'd never been much of a sportsman in the classic way, he did have on the wall a taxidermied sailfish that was more than six feet long. He'd caught it while on a vacation and was proud enough to pay for its mounting.

On the desk were papers beneath a glass weight, a stapler, many books with heavy titles like *Thermionic Phenomena* and a wooden letter opener I'd carved for him in a class when I was young. I remember the arts and crafts teacher had a whole bunch of sandpaper sheets, going from rough to fine. I spent the most time sanding out of the whole class because I wanted mine to feel not like wood but like satin. I wanted to show my father how nice I could make something. I burst out crying when I saw it, kept in pride of place all these years on.

The couch was beneath the fish so that when I lay down I could see the shiny blue underside of what was once a living creature. Its long swordlike nose pointed to the back wall of the room where my father's diplomas and service awards hung. I fell asleep and stayed that way for twelve hours until Jeanie knocked on the outer door to make sure I was all right.

Let me now praise the government man, who was my father. Let me tell the story as he wrote it in his journals. Let me now retell what he wrote so that he is not lost completely.

My father was born one day in January to a woman named Hilde Jensen. A thing I know of Hilde, my grandmother, is that her family was so poor they had to pad their quilts with old newspapers rather than cloth. Hilde married a man by the name of Jesse James. He was not the famous bank robber, but just a farmer from Kansas. I know Hilde died giving birth to my father's younger brother, leaving her oldest daughter, my aunt Marie, to act as an ersatz mother to my father and his baby brother, until Jesse James remarried.

Their world of Kansas was one of the thresher and the cotton gin, rustling fields and dust clouds of biblical heights. My father was raised to know rifles for hunting rabbits. He knew that whips and ropes and every kind of tool hung in their proper places in an area of the barn. In their Kansas people knew that ghosts from unmarked graves haunted the empty lot beside the general store, but they didn't like discussing that.

One of my grandfather's people invented a hay-binding machine, which made them for a time a bit more well off than they would have been otherwise. To figure out the mechanism, the young inventor who was my ancestor lay on his back so he could watch how his mother's hands moved when she knit. Twist and hook and twist again around the needles. He made the machine to imitate human movements with steel fingers at the end of mechanical arms. My father's people had that knack for understanding diagrams and parts and what should come next.

The patent of the machine made the family rich enough to send some sons to college. They went to an agricultural college, but that's still college and therefore powerful. My grandfather went to college so his son did as well. Hilde of course had not gone to college and neither did Aunt Marie. There was nothing unusual about that.

They say that even as a young child my father showed technical cleverness, as if touched by the hand of a machine god. At five years old he took apart a broken clock and then reassembled it so that it worked. He had a love for the logic of parts, precisely aligned.

As soon as my father was taught a theory, he grasped it. He saw in nature the forces described in his science books and that excited him. When he looked at the periodic table the page vibrated like an illuminated manuscript. Those charts and tables that tortured other kids' brains enticed him on. Regular objects were made of particles that moved fast or slow and those could be written down as numbers that communicated qualities or states. They could be stable or unstable.

If you work hard enough, his teachers told him, you could end up anywhere. He could do anything.

At fifteen he was admitted to the Kansas State College of Agriculture and Applied Science in Manhattan, Kansas. There, he studied advanced math, and then engineering. He was moved up the ladder and out of state so he could learn theoretical physics in Chicago. A wonderful progression.

My father worked at Stanford, then for the government at the Hanford site. Then he was brought to Los Alamos. He was a junior man, he worked under Italian, Hungarian, and British scientists recruited for this great project. He learned from German physicists who'd made deals with the American government, who'd fled their homes in the night and moved through foreign lands dragging notebooks and wives. These men sported eccentric outfits in New Mexico, half cowboy, half old-world tutor. I remember them, these men in jeans and neckerchiefs, thick glasses and tweeds and big boots for the mud. Sons of industrialists and rabbis, farmers and professors roughing it in their mountain hideaway, set to save the world by creating the biggest bomb. That's what they believed, I guess. Many mythologies hung in the air at the same time then.

My father idolized foreigners who could solve problems. They gathered together for meetings and colloquia. They drew on chalkboards diagrams of mirrors and the logistics of particles bouncing back. How does an atom rebound? He belonged to a great and terrible project. These men were driven by a great sense of purpose and usefulness. He saw a line stretching back, generation by generation to the enlightenment and before, connecting all the men who wanted to know.

He was plucked out of his common form of obscurity and brought into a secret order devoted to mechanical and chemical magic because his brain could withstand the dissonance. They were sorcerers who bent light and broke apart atoms. Their light could be as hot as the sun. He would bristle to hear me call his work magic, because the men devoted to unlocking atomic power had to believe they were not involved in a mystical pursuit. Part of their religion was to deny the irrational, even as they themselves descended into manias, sometimes to return. The nature of atoms was hovering there, at the edge of their consciousness, they wanted to get ahold of it.

The bomb was dropped. We all know that. The men in Los Alamos could tell you how the Hiroshima bomb had a gun-type detonator with a uranium core while the Nagasaki one was an implosion device with a plutonium core. The difference between them the scientists could describe. It was for others to speak about the implications.

After my mother's death, my father rejected emotional intensity in favor of clean capability. As a living reminder of the radioactive murk of depression and despair, I was too much and so I was kept by Aunt Marie, at a safe distance.

Later, when the volatile pain had been contained by layers of lead, my father married Jeanie, a woman who could maintain a nice life. She kept her slacks crisp. Her pearl necklace hung around her neck. They played doubles tennis on Sunday mornings and had an old-fashioned and coffee afterward at Morning Glory Donuts.

The government gave him, at some point, a plaque for excellence. It is an etched piece of silver-colored metal mounted on a piece of smooth wood. I have it as a memento of all that he did.

Of all the centuries, my father was born into this one. He had appeared as a baby in the olden days and by the time he died, the sky was speckled with satellites. He was smart. He understood. Intelligence flickered in him, soft like the glow of an oil lamp. Abstract solutions flashed in him, bright like a bomb detonating. He worked until his death at the lab.

He is survived by one daughter and she is me.

At my father's memorial his friends praised his diamond-hard mind. The men wore button-up shirts and slacks. Most had the thick glasses you'd expect. No one stood on ceremony or gave any speeches.

We were there to remember and be together, Jeanie said. There were flowers, white carnations and daisies, and some mixed bouquets with the color schemes of purples and pinks. Each one was modest except the one Lev had ordered, which looked baroque and beautiful, but out of place. I had the feeling unshowy, ordinary flowers were the right communication in the town.

An old man said he remembered me when I was little. He had attended my mother's funeral and worked with my father all this time. They'd played tennis together. I recounted a time when my father held my arm to teach me a backhand stroke. But I never committed to the game like he did.

To another couple who knew him and Jeanie, I described my father's lessons about the value of a dollar, and the importance of hard work. I told them my memories of playing in the canyons with the other kids. We had a rope swing that went out into space and then came back. They laughed that everyone was taking risks when the hill was in its early days. The talk felt indefinite. My father could have been any one of them. But maybe that was less a factor of unoriginality than it was of their unity in this town. It felt they all had been to a great and everlasting camp together. Old Eagle Scouts or conference goers in the woods. They were bonded by field and way of life.

I did not share my memories of my mother crying after my father went to work every day of the week. I said I'd lived with my aunt in Colorado during high school because the school was good and my father's career was less certain then. Aunt Marie gave me a sense of security. Of my life, they said that my father was proud of my artistic pursuits. I said I knew, and he was so kind.

I listened to Greg as he described my father helping him with his chemistry homework, but also taking him and Jeanie on long hikes into the Sandias. There was that time seeing the bear and weren't they glad they were riding their bikes when it happened?

Jeanie held up well. She was calm and remained busy. Even though I tried to clear food away and replace napkins and glasses she kept her eye on the liverwurst sandwiches, the radish and butter sandwiches. Her sister had prepared vegetable trays. Her friends had come with plates of deviled eggs dusted with paprika. They brought casseroles and brownies and individual cheesecakes baked in cupcake liners with Nilla Wafers as the crust.

I took a walk on the long cul-de-sac that ran along the mesa's edge. It was all built up now, nothing like the military camp I remembered from childhood. Now where were bright bungalows,

A-frames, and traditional hacienda-style homes side by side. The people here loved the pueblo revival architecture but also a kind of ski town style. The street had a sampler platter of design moving from Sweden to Taos in the span of a lot.

The speed limits here were low to keep children safe. It was before dinnertime so a lot of children were outside, riding their bikes up and down and playing in their front yards beneath pine trees. It was a Friday, so their fathers were probably all still at work at the lab.

The sun was in its descent. The air was warm and soft, it smelled of juniper mainly. I reached the end of the cul-de-sac. I was arguing with no one, crying as I did. The thin air up here could trick a person into thinking the most insane proposition was reasonable, necessary. A piñon tree stood by itself on the cliff's edge. Above, far above the mountains, sunlight pierced through the pink-hearted sunset clouds.

I woke up wrapped tight in the duvet all white. I noticed right away my nostrils were blocked and my teeth hurt horribly. I spit blood into an empty cup on the bedside table. I was back in the maid's room, in Lev's apartment. It was cold outside. It is always cold in one place and hot in another.

I turned away from the tiny arrows of light that were flying through the window and piercing my eyes. Something down on the street was shaking, the industrial-size noise of construction or demolition usual to the city on a Monday morning. I extended one hand from under the blanket, it had its own little tremor. I had a hard time parsing the component parts of the morning, distinguishing the inside from out, my nervous system from the realities of the day.

Is any disturbance ever personal, wholly discreet? People say yes, of course. How you feel does not dictate collective reality. There's such a thing as the impersonal universe. They say that, but I can't help but wonder. What about thread-fine interconnection? Butterflies flapping their powdery wings? When I was young my father had explained to me in a basic way reverberation, particles, and waves, and I absorbed what he'd said. I'm not dumb, like they say.

Since the war the problem has been making sense of life. That's what people say, too. If it all comes down to problems of women and children, guns and men, animals and cells, radiation and extermination, the whole impersonal churn, then what keeps us from offing ourselves? What are the stories we can count on? You can't put the genie back in the bottle. The difference between this Cold War and a hot one is only a matter of where you're living. I know what napalm does to the skin. I've seen real bombs and I've seen pretend explosions and they look the same on-screen. Once it was dropped, the atomic bomb never stopped mushrooming. Even with closed eyes I can see it billowing up and up. What rains down is fine and deadly. In the event of thermonuclear war most will die immediately and the ones that don't will wish they had.

It's difficult to explain. I knew I was cracking up. My father was dead and I wanted to be alone and then Lev went away and I was.

I'd rise late in the morning, wander in circles all day, then I'd go back to bed where I'd stay for ten, twelve, or even thirteen hours. Frittering my life might be a way of describing it.

Lev was filming with Peter in Carefree, Arizona. He would be working for a few more weeks at least. The best thing I ever did was marry a man who didn't want to destroy me. He always let me be, but too much loneliness, just as with too much control, can unhinge a girl. I had wanted this, some time to think. Be careful what you wish for, I told myself, as I tried on all my clothes and imagined situations where I might be seen in each outfit. My loneliness was wearing me down to a stub.

I had been sleeping in the maid's room because ours felt too large. This narrow twin wore white sheets printed with a pattern of pink roses, green leaves, and thorny stems. They were left over bedding from when Iris was a girl, from when Lev was still a family man. I got to be his daughter and servant both in my fantasy.

My mother once told me about how my grandmother was a maid when she first arrived in New York. She got her job at Hotel McAlpin on Broadway because Karla's neighbor worked there, and I assume, because she was white and pretty. Even with practically no English, she always had those things going for her here. In my imagination my unskilled grandmother practiced speaking with the other maids as they folded and smoothed piles of sheets and towels. She was a hard worker, always dead on her feet yet unceasingly active because she had my mother to provide for, who was just a girl then. I picture my grandmother shying away from grasping hands. The customer always has the right to harass. I imagine my grandmother glowing with a practically radioactive desire to change her situation. In America that's what you're supposed to do, the other option being perish.

My grandmother told my mother the hotel was nice. The Americans stayed busy enjoying themselves. Young men insane from the first war smoked in the bar. The hotel was huge and had rooms for parties. A movie star once hosted a private affair for three hundred of his dearest. It was western themed, so hay bales were brought in and a grand, gold-colored, cow-shaped serving vessel was placed upon a table surrounded by fruits and flowers. There were spigots in place of teats and the whole beast was filled with a strong punch. The movie star lay underneath letting the liquor flow straight into his mouth for a laugh.

My mother had so many stories like this. She told them to Renata and to random women like the checkout lady at the grocery store. I overheard. She told them to me and I didn't know how to help her. They had trickled out of her and collected in me. Little pitchers have big ears as the saying goes. I coughed up my mother's liquid stories at the strangest times. It felt like I'd almost drowned years ago but was still expelling the water.

Lev phoned when I was in bed, remembering. He and Peter were going to shoot some scenes in the desert. He wasn't sure when he'd be able to call again. But, Lev said, I have some exciting news. I met a man who wants to direct you in a western. His name is Tony. I told him you're brilliant and he said you have that reputation. I gave him the home number. He's gonna call you. They're about to start film out in Colorado. They have no money. Who does? But they do have Jake Doherty as your co-star.

I listened to Lev's husky voice. It traveled across such a great distance yet arrived into my head as an intimate whisper. I began to cry. I said, I miss you. He said he'd be back soon. I had wanted this, some time to think. Be careful what you wish for, I told myself.

After we hung up the neighbors started arguing and their duet of frustration reverberated the air shaft. We live within clanging voices hardened by past wounds, reperformed in the present. Rehearsal makes it stick. It's live theater with old scripts. It's your imagination, he said. I can't take your constant picking, picking, picking. If you have something you want to say, just come out with it. Why do you always try to provoke me, the man asked. It's as if you want me to hurt you.

When we are babies we don't know our parents as people, we know them as reality itself. We know their most intimate selves, how they smell and taste, the volume of their voices. But it's only later we can begin to see their historic selves, what they might look like without our smudgy wet body of need.

Since my father has died, I've been trying to think about what he did and where he came from. He worked on a project the whole world has opinions about. It makes my thinking hard because the thing is too much. It's hard to look and impossible to turn away.

In a rough draft of the bomb, the scientists experimented with something they nicknamed the demon core. They knew, even as they built around it a joke to cope, that they were reaching down toward the apocalypse. One day a scientist who was filled with too much casual bravado laid his hand on the core. It was an accident. And even though he touched it for only a fraction of a second, it was enough. His skin fell away and soon enough he died in agony.

What they worked on was too much for human touch. Turn away said the natural world, but they could not. It was as if they were driven by an otherworldly power.

The man who was my father worked on tricky small parts of this grand and horrific project. He belonged to a team that devised an inner reflective surface. To get a reaction the energy in the bomb that wants to get out must be turned back in on itself with the aid of a mirror surface. I picture a disco ball turned inside out, though I know that's not it. The bomb had to have an inner life. Only through self-reflection could the chain reaction begin and get going enough to force the full explosion. All this happens in the blink of an eye and then life all around it is torn apart in a flash of blinding light.

Books tell me a story. They said that because the first war was not really settled the second happened. And because the second ended the way it did, other wars after were practically inevitable. The century is a continuous unspooling from how they described it.

I know somewhere in that indefinite span between these wars something happened to my mother that she could not withstand. I imagine a solemn girl doing her chores in the blinding white sunshine among the succulents and bushes of a California yard. In these war times my mother had a father figure. He was a man-shaped sack stuffed with German shrapnel. He raised his hand. Puppetlike, his hand was raised for him. He touched with an open hand, he touched with all his parts in blackout drunkenness. The somber girl remained all the rest of her life touched. She had been flayed from the inside, but you couldn't see by the look of her.

My grandmother called my mother a whore. She was just a child. But I imagine my grandmother called her that because her rage had to fly somewhere and could not hit the target it wanted. What can't a girl's body absorb?

What takes a long time to build can fall apart quick. What is poisoned may stay poisoned for generations to come. After all, from today's magazines and papers we can learn so much, half-lives and cancer clusters, contaminated zones and battles coming back to veterans in their nightmares. You can't remove radiation once it's passed through a body. The cells will bear the mark. How much does it really take to start a reaction? Not much. We are coated in a light, sticky dust. A film has settled over all of us. I have cried too much. Cried because I ceased to know what I was doing. I had the feeling life was polluted. I felt suddenly old.

My father would say, if he could say, I'm getting the science and the politics all wrong. I'm mingling them together willy-nilly. Only thing is, I don't care because I'm an actress, which has sometimes been another word for whore. I like metaphors and images, my body and myths. The country has been at war since the beginning. That much I know. And girls in war cannot be accounted for.

I called out, Mama. She heard the voice coming from another direction, thrown from the past. She was looking for my father, but he was away. He was up high in the mountains. I kept calling but she didn't hear. I could never reach my parents, father or mother. We were separated by heaped sacks, by heaps of bodies. Even still, I never felt a love as complete as what she gave. Even still, in these rose-printed sheets, I yearned for her embrace.

I stopped the house cleaner from coming to the apartment on her weekly visit because I wanted to hang around dressed only in my slip and play my favorite records without interruption.

My favorite singers those days, the only ones I could bear, really, were disappointments like me. I needed to find people who were performing through their funks. They had religions recently acquired, post-divorce hoarseness, drug regrets, and other non-heroic hurts. The records I liked best then were made by great talents out of phase. You could hear them grown-up and over-grown. Rangy is a word for it. They had lost some of their youthful spiritual perfection. They made songs that disappointed fans and critics. Those were the records I played. Miles and Bob, Nina and Joni, you could hear frustration and searching. Can you take my noise, they asked. Can you enjoy my long-winded fury? I will not be taking requests. I will not play the hits. They talked onstage, argued with technicians and scolded the audiences. They left those struggles on the recording for everyone to hear. They dared us to enjoy them in their tangled middle years. This was then the only music I could bear, live recordings.

In the closet corner a pair of Lev's socks huddled, fearful gray baby bunnies. On the dresser my change purse gaped with a wide-open mouth. A feather in the ashtray fluttered its lightest tendrils. In the bathroom someone had left a safety razor blade loose on the windowsill. I looked but did not touch because naked blades are dangerous. Someone should take care of that, of me.

It's fine to swan around the apartment crying and smoking, I told myself. It's fine to eat raspberry jam on a single slice of toast, triangulated with a knife every day of the week. It's fine to have habits. I twirled my seltzer with a lemon peel to make the glass fancy. I had all that and a pot of coffee and that was all I had.

The kitchen table was sunshine-yellow Formica. Lev's wife Grace had chosen this table. I just sat at it. Here I was, sweeping the crumbs off yet another thing chosen by the dead. Scampering from one empty room to another to flip the record back to its original side. Rearranging deck chairs on the Titanic, is that the phrase?

I phoned Suzanna to tell her about things I'd been reading and remembering. There was this one newspaper article I read years ago but some of the details were coming to me now. There were these baby monkeys you see? As an experiment they were deprived of contact with their mothers. First the babies were put in cages alone, and the stress of solitude caused them to walk in endless circles and hurt themselves. Then, when the babies were brought back into monkey society they didn't know how to act. Some of them even died because they would not eat. There was more, I said, about the babies getting surrogate mothers of cloth or wire. Cozy mothers and hard mothers. That was the real point of the article, if I remember correctly. How babies would cling to anything mother shaped, but I got stuck on the babies who stopped eating even when back among their kind.

You know I had my aunt Marie, I had all kinds of care, but also I didn't have my mother and maybe that's why I am as I am.

Suzanna said why don't we get together, honey. I can tell you're having a hard time. Can we have lunch? I thought yes, I should go out. This is too much. I could not stay home indefinitely. Okay, I said. I'll meet you at two. Because the assured voice on the WNEW said it would be brisk and clear all day, I dressed myself in a coat of seasons past to protect myself from the breezes of the present. I circled the house three more times ritually, wrapped a paisley scarf over my hair, and applied a final defensive line of color across my trembling mouth.

An element of film I've always found alluring and terrifying is its continual forward motion. Sure, there can be flashbacks, slow motion, and screens split between different realities, but the film strip itself always spools forward at twenty-four frames per second, the same number as hours in the day. I think progress, historically speaking, is a scam, but our lives do feel as if they roll along on a reel, ever forward.

My sweater beneath my coat felt too tight around my armpits. My skin was hot in the places covered and cold where the air hit. I thought about where I came from and what I should do with myself.

At Lincoln Center I sat down to rest at the fountain's edge. The black circle was the hub of the plaza's wheel, bordered by the opera, the concert hall, the ballet and the wine-dark flow of Ninth Avenue traffic. The water spouted off vertically behind me while people circled around over the unmoving spokes of the gray stone.

Though some don't care for the design and say so at cocktail parties I have always been pleased by these cream-colored monuments to culture. It is our American, slightly cartoon version of Athenian temples. A girl needs a temple and these are the only ones I felt I had a right to.

In my imagination, my impeccably dressed mother shook her head. She was both alive and not, standing beside some western ruins. She was in the remains of a round building, red brown earth and beams, now broken. It was a building dug into the ground. We'd been there before.

Window washers were cleaning the opera's expanses of glass. Standing high up on their suspended board they wiped their squeegees back and forth rhythmically. An old man in a gray suit limped slightly as he passed by heading toward the upper, more western side of the plaza. He disappeared. A young boy was holding his crotch protectively with one hand and on to his nanny's coat sleeve with the other. She was explaining something serious to him but by the expression I could tell he was elsewhere. A woman in a brown leather coat walked by, arm in arm with a friend in a turquoise jacket. They looked so young and happy.

A woman with a Jackie Onassis kind of slimness and wealth entered the scene. It is a wonder of this city that she might be the original just as likely as an imitator. In this city you might catch sight of a messenger sent from another realm, politics or music or art, trying to hail a cab. These icons might have on an ugly raincoat or have some spinach between their teeth. It could happen. Famous people lived here and were sad just like the rest of us. What a thrill. I tried determining if it really was her behind those big dark Nina Ricci's. The whole picture, her fitted trench and slim pants inclined me toward believing it was our genuine lady of national sorrow and riches. I got excited. Her coat was elegant. I was suddenly fixated. Hers was a fame and a pathos I could not resist. For a few more moments I felt a growing thrill. I was her.

At the corner she stopped and turned her. I was let down. It was not the genuine being, just some wealthy woman lost in imitation. Weren't we all? The mimic Jackie caught a cab and disappeared into it. The cab then lost itself in the downstream motion of traffic.

Some stars, who have been compressed into shining beings by the pressure of a million eyes, they really do have something special. They appear far away, even when seen up close. Lev knows famous people, and I've met them. I have found many sad up close, even with or perhaps because of all the charisma. I've recognized in them, because I've suffered from it too, some desperation of character that compels them to perform. There is a willingness to do too much, anything. From a distance it's mesmerizing, like athletes who throw their bodies farther and harder, but up close this special trait is unbearable, or just tragic. I've never cared about fame so much as I've wanted disappearance.

It was time to go downtown to meet Suzanna. I got up but left my silk scarf behind. It was one that had been my mother's. I loved the look of the burnt umber and aquamarine pattern against the black marble. I liked the idea of another person picking it up and taking it home. I've never been good at letting go. The only way I could was on a whim.

Lev knocked on the maid's door and I rose from bed.

He had returned home and I was back from the dead. Nothing was better but time had passed. Darling, he said, you've grown so thin. He held me and we rocked back and forth in one another's arms and it felt so good.

The fridge was stocked. I had ordered groceries and called the cleaner to come and sweep away all evidence of my degradation. He couldn't bear the silence of the apartment and neither could I. He wanted people over for a party like old times. He wanted to chop it up. Out of the Rolodex tumbled numbers. My favorite pieces were freshly laundered and hanging in the bedroom closet. I got dressed carefully. I was preparing for a brand-new scene.

In the hall I arranged things to greet guests as they entered: stargazer lilies radiating out of the mouth of a black vase, sandalwood incense billowing in an atmospheric cloud. Come in, come on in. Extended hands proffered bottles of wine and liquor, bouquets, grapes and fancy cheeses from the market. You didn't need to bring this, we have so much. It's just a token.

The maid's bed got heaped with visitors' coats. A version of me lay under there somewhere, pressed down by strange houndstooths and leathers.

Lev always reminded me through his habits, that existing was not about solutions but rather process and enjoyment. Take your time, he said. It's all we have, these rises and falls. I waved guests toward the kitchen where there was ample ice and glasses and knives for the lemons.

People said I looked terrific, just terrific. What has it been? A hundred years? A thousand? I wore a lavender number cut in a deep V.

Lev had stories from the desert. Have you ever been? Jeez, it's a fantastic place to shoot if you don't mind calamity. Maybe it was our problem. One actor got his nose broken. I didn't have anything to do with that, but a local's jealous husband sure did. There's a physical danger to flirting in small-town bars, that makes it all the sweeter. Another actress got pregnant and our key grip fell from a boulder. He didn't break anything, thank God, but he did need fifteen stitches and there was only a veterinarian to sew them. On the last night everyone got food poisoning and we nearly missed our flights out.

I kept saying, it's okay with me, like I was Elliott Gould playing Marlowe. What a great picture that was. Am I right? It was okay by me on the one hand but also I'll be damned if I didn't get myself an ulcer. Lev held his stomach and said maybe he should be drinking milk but then asked if someone wouldn't pour him another vodka soda. Be a dear?

Oh honey, could you pick out a record? I played a song I'd wept to not days before, but now I laughed and sang along. I draped my arm around Suzanna's shoulder. Peter spilled his wine. Don't worry about that throw pillow, I never liked it.

Nothing was resolved, only softened by the presence of the ones I loved. Lev swung a leg over the side of the couch. We caught each other's eye.

Does anyone need anything?

Acknowledgments

Deepest gratitude to Emily Bell, Allison Devereux, Alexis Nowicki, and everyone at Astra House. Thank you Deborah Ghim. Thanks to Malcolm Sutton, Britt Landry, and Jay and Hazel Millar at Book*Hug. Gratitude to Erin Robinsong, Erin Dowding, Stephanie Acosta, David Geer, Isaac Pool, Tricia Middleton, Mary Marge Locker, Coco Picard, Jake Byrne, Aaron Peck, Eugene Lim, and Jacob Wren. Thanks to Andy Matinog, Maya Matinog, Radhashiri, and the shadow yoga community. Sincere thanks to Edwardo Cassina, Giulia Loli, Shehab Hamad for his great generosity, and everyone who made my time at Kizikula in Zanzibar so consciousness-changing. Endless thanks to Ariana Reines and the Invisible College community. This book a product of that mystical and inspiring school. Love to Geri Murphy, Jessie Hazard, Opal and Ruby Campbell, and the Blevins family. With love and gratitude to Rob Callaghan. In memory of Bruce Blevins.

List of Photographs

Street between Edgehill Road & Whitney Avenue, Hamden, New Haven County, CT, Library of Congress Prints & Photographs Division. Reproduction number HAER CT-186-B-7.

111. Toni Frissell, *A couple walking along the Seine River in Paris,* Library of Congress, Prints & Photographs Division, Toni Frissell Photograph Collection. Reproduction number LC-F9-1964-03-14.

123. Toni Frissell, *Fashion model on edge of boat, man rowing, Montego Bay, Jamaica,* Library of Congress, Prints & Photographs Division, Toni Frissell Photograph Collection. Reproduction number LC-DIG-ds-07071.

143. *Refugees in front of the ruins of the temple of Thesus,* Library of Congress, Prints & Photographs Division, American National Red Cross photograph collection. Reproduction number LC-USZ62-139256.

157. Bernard Gotfryd, *Spectators taking photographs at Tomb of John F. Kennedy. Arlington National Cemetery,* Library of Congress, Prints & Photographs Division, Bernard Gotfryd photograph collection. Reproduction number LC-DIG-gtfy-08762.

175. *"Modesty Blaise" film by American Joseph Losey. Filming in Amsterdam. Monica Vitti and co-star Terence Stamp,* National Archives of the Netherlands, Anefo collection. Component number 917-9565.

193. Toni Frissell, *Swiss Alps Flower Detail,* Library of Congress, Prints & Photographs Division, Toni Frissell Photograph Collection. Reproduction number LC-DIG-tofr-34898.

211. *Cannes. View from the American Red Cross headquarters on the water-front at sunset,* Library of Congress, Prints & Photographs Division, American National Red Cross Collection. Reproduction number LC-DIG-anrc-18770.

223. *Stand of Aspen Trees in Southern Colorado,* author's family photograph.

239. Angelo Rizzuto, *Unidentified woman and Her Reflection,* Library of Congress Prints and Photographs Division, Anthony Angel Collection. Reproduction number LC-DIG-ppmsca-70564.

Photo credit: Justine Kurland

About the Author

Joni Murphy is a writer from New Mexico who lives in New York City. Her debut novel, *Double Teenage*, was published in 2016. It was named one of the *Globe and Mail*'s 100 Best Books of the year. Her second novel, *Talking Animals*, was published in 2020 by FSG Originals.